Best wishes
and aloha,
Kate H Winter

Lost Twain

A NOVEL OF HAWAI'I

Kate H Winter

Outskirts Press, Inc.
Denver, Colorado

This is a work of fiction. The events and characters described herein are imaginary and are not intended to refer to specific places or living persons. The opinions expressed in this manuscript are solely the opinions of the author and do not represent the opinions or thoughts of the publisher. The author has represented and warranted full ownership and/or legal right to publish all the materials in this book.

Lost Twain
A Novel of Hawai'i

v2.0 r1.0

Outskirts Press, Inc.
http://www.outskirtspress.com

ISBN: 978-1-4327-8180-4

PRINTED IN THE UNITED STATES OF AMERICA

My warmest mahalo and aloha to the people who were there at the genesis of this project and kept me centered and hopeful most of the time: Bob Miner whose brilliant idea it was to take scholarly speculation and turn it into fiction; Elaine Handley whose unfailing belief in my work kept me at it; Michael Kiskis who died too soon to read this but whose voice was always with me; JR who keeps me rooted in the history, land and people of Hawai'i with his aloha.

Finally, this book is dedicated to my son Jeffrey Hughs Winter. As a writer and teacher, he inspires me. As a thinker and spiritual warrior, he keeps me faithful to what it is I want to say. As a son, he affirms my choice of this crazy writing life.

Two days ago, the serrated tops of the West Maui Mountains had risen up to meet her as the plane finessed the final approach. Haleakala Crater was just visible through a cloud veil on the other side of the plane's window. In the seat beside her, the woman with skin like brown silk had pulled almost imperceptibly away from contact, straining slightly not to touch Emily's sleeve or her bare arm, not out of any particular fastidiousness but from a well-deserved distrust of *haole* women, white women, in mainland clothes who arrived here in these islands. Emily Witt tried to smile, but she could think of nothing to say, not even some vague pleasantry about the flight. She winced, realizing again how distant from what she thought of as "regular people" her advanced education and the practice of being a professor had made her.

The blond flight attendant had stood somewhere in the front of the plane and came to them as a disembodied voice. "Ladies and gentlemen: once again, science and technology have triumphed over myth and superstition - we have found Maui." Emily pursed her lips in distaste for that kind of pandering to tourists and wondered at the idea of "finding" Maui, hoping that what she sought would indeed be here, on this farthest out bit of land, this "paradise," the islands she had been born in but never really lived on, being an often-transplanted child of the military.

Noting the shared dislike of the stewardess's remark, the woman she had sat silently next to for the eight hour flight from Chicago had ventured a first familiarity. "You arc traveling alone all this way?" The lilt in her voice softened the question. Emily took her first long look at the woman, enough to see the pewter hair waving over her shoulders in - Emily thought - a rather too sensuous way for a woman of her age and ample size.

"Yes."

"You have family on Maui?"

Emily suspected the woman was not really interested, merely excited with finally being at the end of the flight and unable to contain the impulse to connection, even with this taut stranger. Emily had bristled slightly. "No. I was born in Hawai'i - my father was military. We left when I was a baby, and we never came back." That felt like too much to tell this stranger. During the flight, she had watched the other passengers mingle with each other, breaching the barriers that people on other flights usually erect, instead making instant friendships in this community of eager pilgrims to paradise. As well-traveled as Emily was, used to jetting around the world to conferences and academic gatherings, she had long ago acquired the habit of in-flight solitude and practiced it with determination. That had seemed just fine with the Hawaiian woman seated next to her. Now everyone aboard chattered with that same energy of anticipation, but Emily resisted a peculiar urge to tell this woman what it was that she was going to Maui to find. She smothered the information as if starting to tell might lead her to telling things she still had not even said to herself.

She might have said "Herman Melville brought me here" and savored the look of surprise or dismay that would surely ensue. It was mostly true. Herman Melville *had* brought her here. Like all junior professors running on the tenure track, she had been continually on the lookout for a new angle on an old subject, something to write about to put another line on the list of publications that would get her promoted. The habit persisted even now, but tenure wasn't enough, and she had found herself sinking into ennui about her work since it had been granted. Suddenly the campus had seemed very small and the people equally narrow. After six years of negotiating the politics of the department and working at her research and teaching and being assigned to too many committees, it struck her that now that she was tenured, she would never be able to move - that those people and that campus were where she would spend the rest of her life. It took the pleasure out of the fact that she would always have a job to know that it was not a job she wanted.

So, having done what was expected and necessary

for a scholar in American literature, she was casting about for some interesting, arcane bit of news she could research and embellish into an article, perhaps a book. That's when the obscure repartee between Melville and Nathaniel Hawthorne had leapt off the page at her, just a glancing reference, really, to Lahaina, Maui and some obscene adventure Melville had witnessed there. A quick search of the usual sources told her no one else was tracking this story, and she claimed it as her own. The rest of the term she had been quietly ferreting out the details around Melville's time in Hawaii and convincing various grant agencies to give her the money to spend a month on Maui doing the necessary digging. With her usual precision and efficiency, she had gotten her tickets, arranged the rental of a modest motel and car and packed the necessary gear. Now her laptop rested beneath the seat in front of her with her leather bag loaded with tape recorder, camera and an assortment of pens. She looked around her, making sure she had left nothing unsecured. As always for Emily Witt, there was something out of place, missing, just noticeable by its absence.

Stepping onto the smooth tiles of the terminal, she was embraced by the heavy air scented with frangipani and ginger and the rain to the south. The airport was essentially without walls except for the glassed-in gate areas, so every walkway opened onto greenery and slanting sun. Back in Buffalo, the early June sun had heated the earth to first flowering and was suddenly sweltering, but here it was simply summer. Emily was glad she had planned her month here before it got hotter. She would be gone by the 5th of July and back to the predictable chill and sizzle of the Northeast's air conditioned summer.

The way down to baggage claim was a jumble of passengers sweating inside their too-heavy travel clothes, pressing along excitedly, some towing cranky children and wobbling suitcases. In the midst of it all, filling the airport walkway, the Hawaiian woman Emily had spent most of a day traveling next to was laughing within a yoke of *lei* piled on top of *lei*, surrounded by a small crowd of family hugging and kissing her, unfazed by the glares of eager tourists trying to get by. She looked over the tops of small heads and her smile fell on Emily before either realized it. Emily hurried on. The door to the women's restroom was clogged and a line had snaked into the hallway, but up ahead, one of those airport last-stop souvenir shops yawned open and she stepped out of the rush to paradise and into its quiet coolness.

As she backed away from the urgent arrivals, she bumped into a wire rack of paperback books. Reaching to stop its lurching turn, her hand fell on a dark blue cover with a portrait of an Hawaiian woman in what Emily recognized as late Victorian dress, a woman of regal bearing staring at her with sad black eyes. *Hawai'i's Last Queen* the cover read. Emily scanned the books on either side and found another photo, this one of Robert

Louis Stevenson draped in a chair alongside some apparently important personage bearing Polynesian features and wearing British military garb. From the cover of the memoir of Stevenson's adventures in Hawai'i, a headline suggested some liason between the tubercular poet and a princess of the islands. It annoyed Emily, and without thinking why, she moved to take the book off the rack and found behind it, as if hidden there out of the order of things, *Mark Twain's Letters from Hawai'i*. The too pink cover bore no photo, only a drawing that looked like someone's idea of Twain. She weighed the book in her hand, turning it over. It hardly seemed possible that she had never, in her five years of graduate school, picked up Twain's letters from the Sandwich Islands. She knew they existed, of course.

Even though she had adopted the stance of academic contention and humorlessness, she had still studied and even taught Twain, but as little as possible, distancing herself from the charges of racism his novels raised. For all their talk of diversity in cultural studies and post-colonial rhetoric, academic life was still a very white space. Now this book's cover annoyed her with its garish color and etched caricature of white-headed Mark Twain with his cigar, the clichéd image all but obscuring the tropical scene behind him, but she could not put it back on the rack. She put the other two books squarely into their places and walked to the counter where a honey-brown girl smiled a well-studied welcome, and Emily paid for the book before pushing it as far down into the deep pocket of her carryon as she could.

From outside the window of the Islander Inn early that second Maui morning, the smell of plumeria blossoms had slipped through the jalousies inviting her to reveries and pleasures she literally could not imagine. She had decided against staying at the historic turn of the century Pioneer Inn with its creaking floors and antique accessories, even though she knew it was precisely the sort of place that a nineteenth century scholar ought to want to stay. Instead she chose the kind of accommodations that residents on an interisland jaunt would pick - clean, efficient, quiet, with rooms looking like any mainland motel except for the basket of plumeria soap and coconut shampoo by the bathroom sink. After almost a day of naps and cautious self-care, her jet lag abated, Emily felt eager to begin the work rather than feel the languid pulse of the morning. Inside her white car, the scent of its newness assaulted her senses that had only just been awakened by the beauties of Maui. The afternoon of arrival, she had sat at the airport rental car parking lot as long as it took for her to learn where every switch and button was and how it worked before pulling out onto the highway. Now, coasting along the road between Lahaina and Kahului, she passed green expanses of spiked pineapple and tasseled sugarcane fields. She pressed the automatic window control and lowered the green-tinted glass a tentative two inches. The air was softer than she had imagined. It blew her short dark hair to one side slightly and moved like fingers along her neck. Keeping her eyes on the unfamiliar highway, she reached confidently for the air conditioning controls and flipped them off.

The turn-off to Kahului came sooner than she'd anticipated, and she missed it, taking the road to Wailuku instead. It was a surprise to her when she passed a K-Mart and the new mall and found herself in front of the Bailey mission house museum. Having spent an unfruitful hour in the Baldwin museum house in the whaling port of Lahaina the previous afternoon, she did not intend to waste any more time listening to the defensive pseudo-history of well-meaning, white-skinned docents who wanted to tell the Christian missionary side of Hawai'i's past. It was more than unlikely that there was anything of worth to her there, certainly nothing connected to her Melville research.

Across the street, the white and green facade of Queen Kaahumanu's church rose trimly above the slope of lawn. It reminded her of every other Congregational church she had seen including the one in Lenox, Massachusetts that she had discovered while searching for the house that Melville had lived in. The building felt familiar, and she could ask directions to get her back on her way. She stepped out of the car and like a reflex gathered her gear bag before closing and locking the door. She walked lightly across the crisp grass, ticking off the facts she had picked up about Maui's oldest stone church – 1830's -- Queen Kaahumanu - Kamehameha's favorite wife – who became a Christian and burned the old idols. One of the heavy double doors of the church opened and a man in a faded blue shirt stepped out, turning back to twist a large old-fashioned key in the clanking lock. As he did so, he saw her and reversed the process, pushing the door wide open instead. He turned to face her as she hesitated near the foot of the church steps.

"Aloha," he called out softly. "I have been expecting you."

She barely took in what he had said. "Were you closing up? I see - it's nearly noon. I only wanted to ask . . . ."

"I know. *E komo mai*. Welcome." He gestured to the open door.

"But I don't want to keep you if it's time for you to close for lunch or . . . ."

"I was expecting you."

"You were?"

"Yes. You are looking for something here."

"Well, not particularly here - well, perhaps." She followed his gesturing hand and slipped past him into the cool interior of the old church. She felt his warmth and took in a faint scent of sandalwood as she edged around him. He stepped inside with her, closing the door behind him.

"Go ahead - look all you like. I will be right here." He sat easily on a hard chair just inside the door, and leaned on the table beside it. With his elbow he pushed aside the small pile of hymnals and Bibles that rested on the starched white cloth and cradled his chin with his palm.

The air inside was light and somehow green, soft with mysterious fragrances and fresh air sailing through the wide high windows. Accustomed as she was to the musty coolness of research libraries and the rather dark interiors of New England churches she had mined for material, this church felt deliciously open, and she was sure it held no secrets, nothing useful. The essential elements of old New England Protestantism were there - the pews in prim rows, stark white walls, the absence of any ornament and display, a barren house where Christianity had been stripped of all color, reduced to only darkness and light and simple rules about them. In a corner of one window, a spider sprawled big as a plate, hunting or resting, she couldn't tell which.

The quiet of the place, and its cool breeziness after the warmth outside, soothed her, and she drifted in it. Gradually she wakened to his presence again and turned to face him. His hand slipped into a bag near his feet and his eyes met hers as he pulled something from concealment. He stood and stepped toward her, both hands stretched before him bearing a *lei* of deep pink plumeria blossoms, clearly intending to put it over her head. When she saw what he held, she inclined her head slightly in an uncharacteristic gesture of submissive acceptance, and he laid the flowers on her neck and shoulders. His face bent near hers, and cheek brushed cheek in the Hawaiian way of greeting.

"Aloha. It is good you are here."

She could say nothing in response. He only smiled at her silence. She knew she should be making some kind of talk to fill the quiet, but nothing came. It seemed the only language she knew was insufficient to this.

"Kamuela," he said as he placed his hand flat and firm in the middle of his chest. It would have been less dismaying to her if he had thrust his hand out to shake hers. Now she saw the large, dark fingers, squared palm and smooth nut-brown skin against his chambray shirt.

"Emily," she responded, finally, resisting the impulse to put her hand on her own chest. "Dr. Emily Witt."

"Is there anything you would like to ask?"

"Oh no - I just wanted to see - it's a superb example of the style . . . ."

"Maybe you would like to come for worship. They have service in Hawaiian."

"I don't speak the language."

"Perhaps it does not matter."

The habit of contention rose in her then, and she looked at him closely, taking in the cinnamon color of his face with its wide Polynesian nose and full, sensuous mouth. But his eyes caught hers. Hazel eyes. Not the dark brown depths of the few local people she had actually taken the time to look at, and not the brooding black eyes that seemed to glare at her at the car rental place. Kamuela's eyes were pale, with glints of green like the light inside a forest and there were streaks of blue like that of his shirt. Definitely hazel.

"I'm here to work - looking for material about Herman Melville. He may have stopped here."

"Melville. I see. Are you not looking for something else as well?" She shook her head in denial. "Ah - then maybe you are not the one."

"The one?"

"The one I was expecting."

"Oh, that's what you meant before. I should have told you then, when you said that. I'm sorry. I didn't mean to mislead you."

He waved off her apology. "Come." She followed him onto the wide lanai and heard the dull clank of the lock behind her. He turned and took her elbow, moving her along creaking planks toward two well-used rattan chairs in the narrow bit of shade at the far end of the lanai. He sat before she did, stretching his legs before him, tilting his head back. The breeze shifted an arm of palm, letting in sun that glinted in his hair, showing up the red tint in it. "Tell me about Melville, please."

At last, something she had comfortably rehearsed. "He was in Lahaina in April 1843 after leaving a whaling ship. He was technically a fugitive, having jumped ship in the south Pacific." She felt the force of his listening and paused, shifting her attention. "I'm an English professor - in New York - and in my research I discovered a place in one of his letters where he mentions an adventure on Maui, and it seemed that no one had written about it yet, so I came out here hoping to turn up - something."

"Why is Melville important to you?"

Framing an answer for this Kamuela who sat so solidly opposite her, an answer that would explain the intricacies of politics in the university's English department - of career-building and competition and pressure to publish - it was just impossible to explain to someone who had perhaps never been to college.

"He isn't, particularly." The truth in her answer surprised her. She had to resist the nagging suspicion that what she did was just a way of securing a job, hack scholarship, without passion. Some days she felt that she was merely part of a vast industry that produced useless essays and books that no one but other workers in the industry were even mildly interested in - reams of polished academic prose too arcane for anyone but academic insiders to bother with. She could not possibly tell him that. "But my work depends on finding a new story, a new slant, some new bit of information about American writers and . . ."

"There are many American writers." He slid his bare foot along a ridge of the floor and back, marking time.

"Yes, but I've already published several pieces on Melville and have some small reputation there." He looked unconvinced. He waited. "And my father often spoke of Hawaii. My family left the islands when I was a baby. My father was stationed here, in the military, and whenever he spoke of it, there was such longing in his voice. I wanted to come and see for myself."

Kamuela took a long breath. "Travelers leave home to find relief from feeling like strangers in their own worlds. Then they discover where it is that they are supposed to be. Some stay. Some return."

Emily didn't see how this pronouncement had anything to do with her. She straightened the pleat in her khaki shorts and sharpened the crease between unpolished fingernails. "I am here to work."

He shook his head in a gesture of disbelief or negation.

"It's late, and I have kept you from something." She apologized but couldn't keep the dismissal out of her voice. She offered her hand to him in a way she intended as business-like. He held it, leaning in to touch her cheek again with his.

"*Ho'i hou* – come back. I will be here again tomorrow. If you come, I have something to show you. Something that will interest Professor Emily Witt."

A restless night and waking long before the sun came up convinced her that at thirty, she wasn't recovering from crossing time zones – six of them – as quickly as she used to. It was too early to do anything but drive, so that next morning she sped across the valley that joins West and East Maui, not missing the turn-off to Kahului this time, and headed out toward the infamous road to Hana. Fifty-six bridges and fifty-three miles of hairpin turns and narrow roadway hacked into the east-facing shoulder of the island made it attractive to tourists who wanted to be able to brag that they had made it to the village of Hana, even though all they would do there is dash into the Hasegawa Store to buy an "I Survived the Road To Hana" t-shirt to verify that they had made it and head back to Kahului or the west side resorts again.

These days, shops in Lahaina sold the shirts too, saving less daring tourists the imagined perils of the trip.

Emily reached the Paia village sign announcing the last stop for gas and food, slipped the CD labeled "Hana Road Tour" into the player in the dashboard and readied herself for a drive that she thought could not be as harrowing as people claimed. The sun was just up and slanting low across the water. Stopped at the last stoplight she would see for hours, she checked again out of habit to be sure her pens and notepad, thermos of coffee and bottle of water were on the passenger seat. Reaching to grab a pen from the leather bag, she tipped it over and had to stuff the aspirin, bandaids and flashlight back inside with the bathing suit and motel towel.

The two-lane road curved along the cut in the hills and past gashes in the red earth for several miles, through rooster towns - villages that had once flourished where now only chickens made a sound. Above her on the right stood Haleakala, the dormant volcanic mountain, its summit free of cloud and magnificently rose-colored in the morning light. Later in the day there would be bumper to bumper rental cars making the trek, but with no tourist traffic out this early, the only people she saw were locals heading toward work in Kahului or the west side resorts, until a tour bus suddenly appeared at her rear bumper silently urging her to either pull over or speed up. The driver was just visible through the windshield, his orange and green aloha shirt like neon through the tinted glass. The road narrowed still more and he continued to press close behind her, pushing her to drive faster than she wanted to. Hana Road switched and shifted ahead of her so that all she could do was drive. The voice on the cassette told her there was a turn-out coming near mile-marker eleven, so as she negotiated a hard curve and dip in the highway, she flipped on her turn signal and pulled onto the cindered parking area that served as trailhead for a waterfall hike. Right behind her, the bus lurched around the curve and eased into the pull-out. A gaggle of tourists stepped off and began the walk to the waterfall as Emily sipped spring water from her bottle. The bus driver languidly stepped down from the bus, cool and detached now that he was without his charges for a few minutes. When she looked up, he smiled at her. When she only stared back at him and didn't return his greeting, he headed around the front of the bus to light up a cigarette. She reversed quickly and headed on again, not eager to make time as much as unwilling to wait for him to leave first to avoid his tailgating.

She passed eight bridges and several precipitous curves along ridges that dropped straight to the ocean before he caught up with her again. She had just barely glimpsed the cascades and shimmering pools etching the recesses of the gulches that were spanned by narrow old bridges where she slowed to let an on-coming pick-up or impatient jeep cross first. Now she felt him behind her and looked for a place to pull over. The voice on the cassette went on uselessly as she hurried through the green around her. A sign on the left announced "Uncle Hari's Fruit Stand" and a wider place along the road's shoulder. Emily swerved into it. As she turned off the car, she heard the whine of the bus's diesel engines go past and smelled the acrid exhaust. She refused to look at the driver.

Below the "Uncle Hari's" sign was a hand-lettered addendum she had not seen at first: "Locals eat here. You should too!" On the back wall of the open shed hung a menu of unappetizing smoothies and local food she couldn't identify, so she drank her coffee and got back on the road, easing into slow mode. The scenery took on definition as she passed, the undulating green differentiated into kukui, bamboo, eucalyptus, and here and there guava and mountain apple hanging heavy on the boughs. She felt her tires slip slightly on the pavement where a heavy fall of mangos had been mashed to pulp by traffic. She leaned into the curve of road, letting her body take the sway. The "highway" arced left, toward the ocean below, until it seemed that if she did not stop, she would go over the cliff and across all that verdure into the place where the surf pummeled the lava. She cruised into a parking area that promised a view, grabbed the thermos and stepped into the morning light. The canopy above and dry duff under her feet quieted the engine hum in her head. She realized that she hadn't put the Hana Road guide back into the player since Uncle Hari's and had no idea where she was. Up the knoll, over the urgent, gnarled roots of eucalyptus, she climbed to a low lava wall that stopped her just before the land dropped away and the coast opened in front of her. The coolness of the trade winds at that elevation made her glad for the coffee. The breeze seemed to come from every direction at once but some insistence in it drew her eye northward. Rain clouds came rolling over the edge of the island toward her, bearing a rain so light that it scarcely penetrated the canopy. All about her the scent of eucalyptus was set free in the dampness. Sun and shadow played against the surly water below her. Trade winds whipped the tops of the waves to froth against the darkest blue water further out. Beneath it all was the insistent surge of surf and closer to shore a pelting rain glooming southward toward Hana.

She heard laughter even above the grind of the truck's transmission as it turned off the highway into the paved parking lot where her rental car sat alone. The black pickup seemed headed for the far side of the lot, as far from her as possible, and she saw its assortment of bumper stickers: "Eddie Would Go" and "Aloha the Aina" and "Hawaii For Hawaiians" was all she could quickly read. It barely stopped before two slim-hipped, muscled local men leapt from the truck bed held high off the ground by monstrous tires. They hoisted coolers and a camp stove out of the back and bore them on their shoulders up the slope to a picnic table she had not even noticed. The others untangled themselves from the clutch of family in the back and handed toddlers down to the young men from the chest-high rear of the truck. They had come for the day. That much seemed clear to her as they laughed loudly and chattered with each other in Hawaiian pidgin she couldn't understand. In no time it seemed they had made a bivouac and set up a camp kitchen. Their high spirits and loud patois made her suspect they were drinking even at that early hour, and she stiffened against the imagined menace in them. Her rain-damp shirt clung to her now, uncomfortable. They barely looked in her direction, but one of the men stepped away from the rest of the group and sauntered toward the same stone wall she occupied, bending to light a cigarette as he went. When he lifted his eyes, he nodded to her, looking hard at her dark hair and the blush of flesh in the open neck of her polo shirt. When she didn't respond, he turned aside. A woman at the picnic table looked up at them as two of the younger men started in the same direction. Emily picked up her bag and moved down-slope, following the lava wall, toward an opening that would let her get back toward the car. Safely inside it, she pulled out of the parking area, hesitating a long time at the edge of the roadway before she turned left, back toward Kahului and away from Hana.

The heat had thoroughly dried her shirt by the time she stopped the car at the curb in front of Kaahumanu Church. Kamuela was stretched in the chair at the far end of the lanai, waiting, it seemed.

She realized she had no reason prepared to explain her coming back again.

He made it easy for her. "Aloha. Come, sit here in the shade awhile," he called down to her. The strength of his raised voice startled her - she remembered a velvet murmur yesterday. But sitting beside him, she felt safe, though she hadn't acknowledged the deep uneasiness she had felt out on the road until now.

"Have you been finding Herman Melville?"

"No." The quiet between them was heavy with scent of plumeria, and she remembered the lei he had given her now draped over the bedstead in her motel room. "I had thought I would go to Hana today." He nodded his head, but not so much in approval as understanding.

"And you're back already?"

"I didn't actually go all the way . . . a tour bus – the road was crowded . . ."

"Hana is fine, but you don't need to go so far to find what you seek." His shaman's manner irritated her vaguely, but she felt comforted somehow sitting near him. Turning slightly, she caught the scent of sandalwood coming from his clothes and took in the cinnamon of his skin where his shirt opened at the throat. He was, she suddenly noted, without hair on his arms and legs, smooth as a shaved woman, and all over he was the color of spice. The noticing surprised her. It had been at least six years, back in graduate school, since she had thought about a man's body that way. The last time had been before she began her teaching position at Buffalo, where all the straight men she met were tweedy or taken or both. The incessant scramble for publication and travel to conferences to give lectures and creating a space for herself in the English department—the insane obsessions of getting tenured—had displaced those other interests and curiosities about a good looking man. And it was too dangerous to start something with a colleague, even one at another campus. Two scholarly careers could not help but contradict each other. It had seemed necessary to simply close off that part of life.

But there sat Kamuela. He reached down into his backpack where it rested by his bare feet and pulled two chilled bottles of mango nectar. "Would you like one?" She said no, and he simply put one of the damp bottles near her feet. He drank as if there was nothing in the world he wanted more in that moment. He looked younger than the thirty-something she had figured him to be at first.

"I am glad you came back."

"You said you had something to interest me."

"I counted on your professional interest." She wondered what other sort of interest he might ascribe to her return but let the thought go. He eased out of the chair and dropped off the edge of the lanai, disappearing around the shaded side of the church. She heard a car door open, then close. When he reappeared, he held a small bundle in front of himself, reverently. He took the long way back to her, climbing the church steps deliberately and crossing to her, standing before her like a supplicant or acolyte.

"This my grandmother gave to me many years ago and told me you would come for it some day." The wrappings began to fall away as he unfolded layer upon layer of *tapa* cloth like soft parchment covered in brown geometric designs. "A week ago, I had a dream of a white bird and you coming for this." In his wide hand lay an old notebook of the kind that men a century ago used for their diaries. The smooth edges of its pages bore a marbled pattern of red and black and what had once been gold. The cover of tan calfskin was stained but not mildewed. It was the sort of artifact that Emily was used to handling in archives and old libraries, but she held back. He silently urged her to take it, then held it while she gently turned back the cover and revealed the first of the blue-lined pages. "April 14, 1866," it read in faded pencil, and then commenced a scrawl that looked as if it would be easier to decipher than many of the 19th century scribbles she had transcribed. Emily lifted her eyes to Kamuela's, surprised at how close he was and the resolution in his face.

"You must read it. Then you will know what to do with it."

"But whose is it?"

"One of my ancestors. The one I took my name from. A *haole* man. You will see."

"Howlie?"

"Ha-ole . . . *haole*, non-Hawaiian."

"You mean white."

"It means much more than that. It is people lacking *ha*, the breath of life – people who are not Hawaiian in their spirit. Outsiders. You will see."

She fingered the page again, feeling a cool dampness on it, confused that it smelled not at all musty as old papers usually did but fresh and vaguely herbal. She turned it over in her hand and a fragrant leaf fell out, then a single sheet of paper that had long been pressed into compact quarters, the edges of each fold fragile from age and the many times it had been read. The paper crackled as Emily opened it again.

Beloved companion,

I regret that there is no word in your language for farewell or goodbye. Aloha is too imprecise, used for greeting and farewell and everything else as it is. Yet maybe it is perfection of language itself, containing as it does the sorrow of going and hope of coming again.

Now I would use aloha in all its many ways to tell you that even as I must leave, I will always be loving you. I will go to bed each evening with aloha on my lips, thinking of you, and wake each morning anticipating the day when I come again to this place and you.

I must go back. The specter of the felt-hat man haunts me. The paper sent him, I'm sure of it. I have not sent a dispatch in over a month. Here with you I have been happy at last, too content to trifle with the world's affairs - easy in the hours, our simple days and nights, loving you as I had never guessed a man might love.

But I must go back. This Eden is your world. Mine lies the other side of beyond. You would wither in mine and I cannot linger here in yours just now. But know that I will come again and find you, my sweet heart, my dearest companion, my love.

I've nothing to leave with you but this notebook. As I look into it, it's full of you and the moon and the bliss of our weeks together.

Keep it. I need nothing to remind me - the memory will be with me every moment that I am away. Aloha nui loa until I come again,

SLC Your Maka

The initials meant nothing to her. Neither did the Hawaiian word "maka."

"Who or what is 'maka'?"

"It means someone held close, a beloved."

Emily folded the page carefully and closed the journal.

"Take it, please. Read it. You will know what to do."

In fact, she had plenty to do - she had an interview tomorrow with the historian from Maui Community College, and she needed to fly over to Honolulu to track down a lead at the Bishop Museum. Yet the weight of the journal in her hand and the scent of *maile* in it and Kamuela's nearness urged her to it. He still stood before her, bent so his head nearly touched hers. It surprised her that she wanted to do this for him.

"Alright."

"*Maika'i*. Good. It is good. *Mahalo*." His hand was warm and firm where it touched her arm. He let it lay.

"Well, I had better get to work," she finally murmured. Neither of them moved.

"Tomorrow I will not be here at the church," he said softly. "My day off. Perhaps you would like to go swimming?"

"I have much to do - an interview tomorrow . . ."

"After that."

"It might be late," she hedged.

"Not too late," he insisted.

"Can I call you?"

"No need. I will find you."

She hugged the *tapa* bundle and headed for the car. The smell of *maile* and old leather filled the interior as she headed back to Lahaina.

Emily sipped the cup of Kona coffee she had brewed in the pot provided in her room and stretched herself on the prickly bed cover. She picked up the antique journal. It was really too hot for either the coffee or the cover. Lahaina town in the summer steamed and sweated until late evening. She put down the leather book and cup, stripped off the bedspread, then her shorts and t-shirt, and lay back in just her panties with the night air ruffling over her skin. Opening the leather cover, she saw that two pages had been torn out, the first two, and not neatly. The scribble began or continued on the third page, and she started to read.

April 14, 1866

Strong coffee and opinions from the reverend this morning - about my being out late with Miss M. of

Ulupalakua Ranch in west Maui. Rode to Kihei and back, returning in the evening. She and her pretty sister are fine horsewomen for kama`aina girls reared up on these mares, but never will compare to the native women on horseback. Ulupalakua means something about ripening breadfruit, but the place is also famous as "Rose Ranch" for its lavish gardens and hospitality – all manner of high-toned visitors, ambassadors, explorers, royalty, even authors! A fine frame for the allure of the owner's daughters. Both are good-looking girls, simply and modestly clad even in Hawai'i's heat, accomplished, heirs to a plantation that yields a respectable $60,000 (annual). Either of the young ladies would make a likely wife, intelligent, well-bred, child of a respectable family, and spotless in reputation, despite riding out with me. This morning's conversation turned to marriage and Miss M's inevitable descent to it. I assured the reverend that I'm an unlikely prospect - no decent clothes and less money - she's after a man with more than a slight reputation as a newspaperman to recommend him! Still, had I been more enterprising and blest with a bit of capital, I'd have had a chance to marry the girl and the plantation and live in upcountry comfort where the whiskey is always top shelf.

Truly the lack of money is the root of all evil.

Mr. K.is a good man despite being a deacon of the church. He has received me with as much consideration as usual from Americans living in the island, and more than a haole Congregationalist generally, enough to keep me from being altogether uncomfortable. There is a certain degree of prestige and social acclaim accorded me as a "writer on assignment" in Honolulu and even here on Maui. The parlors of the island's aristocracy are opened to me. The court, certain politicos, even the children of the original missionaries – now powerfully invested in land and politics – all greet me with respect that is usually reserved for one of their own kind.

But for authentic cordiality and cheerful hospitality, you must visit with the Kanaka. Their Aloha is that old loving-kindness of the Bible. Even missionary families cannot outdo the natives in their generous welcome, whether they are expecting you or not, or have a meal to share or not. They will entertain you delightedly if not extravagantly and sometimes throw in the attentions of a daughter as well! I notice, however, that when a meal is served, the native children are fed first, unlike our way of shoving them off elsewhere for their provisions. It is always so, to insure the survival of the race, an ancient custom from uncertain times.

Having concluded my study of the sugar plantations and Miss M, I was ready to move on. Mr. K. threw open the door and commenced his breakfast sermon just then and the morning fell in. I was to begin the journey to Hana today with some rambunctious youth the reverend Mr. K. had engaged, but now there stood in front of us a woman, youngish, of that better class of Kanaka. She waited. For me, probably. "I am here for Mister C." confirmed it. K. inquired what had happened to her brother and learned that he'd broken a leg the day before, though I couldn't make out precisely how that had happened - it seemed to involve a horse, one of those sway-backed, headstrong and spine-weak mounts that the natives prize. When the consultation before me ended, he turned to me and reassured me that this woman would do as a guide to my next accommodation.

"Surely you don't expect me to go off with her - she's hardly . . . " I protested somewhat feebly, but she was not, I saw, as young as I had supposed at first. Owing to the smoothness of her skin, her diminutive stature and the lithe grace of her body even inside that calico tent the missionaries had legislated, I'd underestimated her by perhaps a decade.

"The native women ride as well as the men. Just follow her and try to do as she tells you."

I looked at her gingerbread skin, those black eyes, an extravagant cascade of dark hair, a perfect island beauty, and reconsidered. "She speaks English?"

"Of course! Educated at the mission school over in Lahaina. Knows the Bible as well as most missionaries." I should have known better than to book a tour with a deacon.

"She won't preach at me, will she?"

He didn't answer me directly. "Napua," my host said with undisguised disdain - for myself. Her name, I supposed he meant.

It was then she raised her eyes to me, and though I mistrusted it, I gave myself into her hands.

The horse she'd brought was the capricious sort of nag I'd learned to loathe in my adventures on Oahu. It jerked the reins and launched left, then right as I approached it. The woman gathered its head in her hands & whispered some Kanaka secret into its muzzle whereupon it settled into a comfortable stance. Having accomplished the saddle, I was bumped about some but felt secure with such an able horsewoman in front of me. She never stopped to look at me without laughing, hiding her mouth behind her hand - to spare my feelings?

We left Wailuku behind. Wailuku - translates to "bloody waters" or "destructive water" or something of the sort from the battle fought at nearby Iao Valley by the first King Kamehameha. Places here are named in the aboriginal way after some natural feature or something that grows in the neighborhood or some noteworthy event that occurred there. I have yet to find any town, crossroads, settlement or watering hole christened with a man's appellation such as we are wont to bestow back in America. The haoles seem content to let the landscape continue wearing these descriptive labels for names instead of smearing their own patronyms all over the map of paradise. There is <u>Lahaina</u>, after a variety of sugarcane that grows there. Many places hereabouts bear names that incorporate those of plants or animals or winds or rains or seas - all kinds of natural features - announcing the general importance of the land and the critters that inhabit it as far as the natives are concerned. Everything is a divinity it seems, even the stones. If you ask what a name means, you are apt to get a romantic tale of lost lovers or a lizard turned to stone by Pele, their ancient vulcan goddess, or some such wondrous event, and begin to suspect that every *inch of this kingdom has had a vivid past - or that these fanciful narratives are invented to divert the inquisitive tourist.*

Then there is Kahului named after a particular array of warriors on the battlefield. In fact, a good many of these majestic places are named for military events, Wailuku being the site of a decisive battle led by their pagan warrior king. The valley might better be remembered for the verdant pinnacle that graces it instead of the blasting cannons that cut the enemy forces to smithereens and made the stream run red. When it was done, the king made another sacrifice of human life to thank his war god Ku. The history of warfare in these islands is more horrid and inhumane than any I've heard of yet. Brutality reigned along with the old despots. The internecine war in our own disunited states is foul enough, but here in this miniature kingdom, where everyone is related to everyone else, it seems a particular travesty of human feeling to be slashing and spearing one's cousins and uncles. The desire to kill folks to whom you have not been introduced propels American soldiers through an uncivil conflict, but here war has a particularly familial aspect.

The woman led the way out of Wailuku town southward toward the shoulder of Haleakala. Having already seen the great crater of the mt. with Miss M. and friends, I was not fooled one moment by the gentle green curve of its flank. From down here, one would never guess at the desolation of cinder and stone up there, a crater big enough to lose Connecticut in, quiet since its last eruption in 1790. Lacking all vegetation, cinder cones thrust upward like Massachusetts hills from the crater's floor. While the colors of the rock, hues from russet to heather, soften the effect somewhat, down here the greens more than compensate for a want of softness up there.

We met a party of four and my guide Napua instructed me to give them a wide berth, abdicating possession of the trail. No greetings were exchanged as they passed - remarkable here where everyone lingers to swap news and lies. This appeared to be two policemen and two miscreants of some kind, tied and well-guarded. One of the men went peacably between the two guards, but the younger one twisted and jerked his arms, resisting the rope bindings about his wrists, tied there, Napua assured me later, only because he had protested his arrest. With a wild look he cast his eye about - it being the only free part of him - looking for a chance of escape. Shoeless and shirtless, with only a ragged pair of white trousers, he would not get far, I suppose. After they disappeared down the trail, she explained that they were two lepers and the health officials who had found them. The "Chinese disease," they call it, claiming it arrived in Hawai'i with them. Last year the legislature passed an act to prevent the spread of the disease and now they have put a government schooner to work hauling any lepers they can find off to a colony on the island of Molokai. It is not the relocation that the lepers resist but leaving their families behind, "ohana" being more important to them than themselves, says Napua.

All the whites fear leprosy dreadfully and treat the sick like niggers, wrenching them from families and friends, all the things that make life dear. Taking the opportunity for moral pronouncement, they blame the scourge on the native custom of sleeping promiscuously and being too generous with their intimate hospitality, which of course gives the haoles *reason to withhold their pity for the sick and toss them on a remote scrap of land to rot and die as Providence decrees. And then those same politicos and police go to church on Sundays and congratulate themselves on their humanity in not just casting the poor rotting souls into the sea. What a Heaven it will be when all those old hypocrites assemble there! I don't think I will care to go.*

Napua tells me it is good fortune or better that there were two victims because meeting one on the trail would have meant some mishap awaited us. How easily her native superstition mingles with her Christianity!

Religion and education are not as sudden as massacre but more deadly to people in the long run. At this rate, with the assorted illnesses outsiders have brought to these natives -- smallpox - measles – diseases of the venereal sort, not to mention what they call Christianity -- the Hawaiian race may die out altogether. The men of the United States of America are doing their share to populate Hawai'i with half-American descendants of merchants and missionaries to compensate for their part in decimating the native race. Day by day, their numbers drop off precipitously and are supplanted by Chinese coolies brought in to work the plantations. The Chinese make excellent hands, and the sooner California follows this kingdom's example and imports coolies, the better. It makes cheap labor for the meanest drudgery - work that no man of intelligence and education is fit for. Naturally I can't put a word of this into the dispatches - bad for business – it would scare off the investors and make room for more missionaries! Though they aren't entirely without value, these clerics - one has volunteered to go to Molokai to care for the lepers – not a Protestant missionary but a priest, according to rumor.

This time on Maui has had a different cast from the very outset. The voyage from Honolulu was fraught with adversity. First - it was a schooner, not a steamboat, and so had no whistle for signal, leaving the crew to ring bells and wildly haloo one another to make known their intentions to other vessels and those on the pier. The front section of the boat was for cabin passengers, while aft was reserved for the native folk traveling with their relatives, dogs, cats, mats, pipes, poi, fleas, cockroaches and all such baggage and accessories necessary for a voyage across the channel. At dusk, I had a cabin to sleep in, but the native passengers simply spread themselves athwart the deck and one another in a sociable tangle and commenced snoring. Now and again a child might whimper and a pair of lovers feign seclusion for an affectionate scuffle, but generally, despite the pitch and roll and glare of moonlight, they all slept deeply like children on an outing. We haole passengers, unaccustomed to the cruder mode of travel above on the deck, expected to be much more comfortable in our narrow bunks, cut off entirely from the bracing air, inches above bilgewater, and nibbled by rats. By the end of first watch, I had given up any attempt at sleep and joined the crowd on deck where the soothing slap of the waves on the schooner's sides soon lulled me into a refreshing slumber.

April 15

Much of today we were riding along a trail that we could sometimes take two abreast though it was muddy and treacherous with braided, tangled tree roots coiled beneath the feet of our good steeds. However serpentine they may at first appear, one quickly eases into the heedless habit of a snakeless paradise and ceases looking about for adders, raising one's eyes to the horizon and heaven instead. The trail is little more than a gash in the side of the mountain, this quiet old volcano called Haleakala (the house of the sun), insistently grown over by the extravagant tropical foliage of every description that one finds here on the windward side. Green-backed Hawaii. And water everywhere - not only the ocean before us but waterfalls, cascades, pools and dripping rain that comes in the evening over the Pacific from America. It is the rain that will water the cane lands. I think I almost catch the scent of money in it - enterprise. That's why they call them trade winds, I suppose.

The greater part of the wealth and commerce here belongs to Americans. They own whaleships, provision and mercantile establishments, sugar plantations, ranches and a brothel or two. Though Americans have the most commercial interests, the English and Europeans are monopolizing the government, having more experience – and a more positive one – with monarchs than the Americans. The best argument for the California steamships is that a trip this way of only 7 days and back to San Francisco in 9 would populate this kingdom with Americans and loosen the grip of the English and French.

Despite their fiduciary power and apparent security, cordiality and good cheer are lacking among most Americans living here - they have lost whatever openness and easy warmth they may have brought with them and become cold and reserved as Boston deacons - frigid, even - distant, suspicious, with a bewildering lack of vivacity and natural sociability. They aren't part of the royal Hawaiian court, and have no truck with the common natives either. You would expect they would have created their own social grazing land by now, isolated as they are from the rest of their civilization - a sort of marooned race! but instead they seem anxious to keep to themselves and adhere strictly to the code of what's proper & due rather than what's inviting. I met the new minister to China, Burlingame, in Honolulu and his advice to me is born of this peculiarity of haoles in Hawai'i. "Avoid inferior folk and seek only the companionship of those superior in intellect and character. Climb!" he exhorted me, if I intend to make my fortune here.

Some of the Americans are making their fortunes neatly. Now that the need for whale oil has dwindled with the discovery of petroleum in Pennsylvania, the number of sugar plantations and mill companies here in the islands has increased three-fold the amount of sugar that's available for export. The ravages of the war in the South need not keep the muscavado and grocery grade sugar off American tables. With three growing seasons in a year's span, these islands can grow an abundance of cane, and Hawaiian sugar is just as fine in quality as California's - or better. All we've got to do is what that bunch at old Jamestown colony did - advertize! Tell 'em back home how lush and ripe the islands are, how easy the natives are to keep happy, and where the $$ is to be made. Write it so the $$ will flow - sell it to them. Until now this kingdom has kept afloat by offering services to whalermen and re-exporting goods for merchants, but now the sandalwood's gone and the old dependency on sea and trade routes is all but replaced by the sweet green gift from Hawaiian soil. There's a great deal of dust and clamor here about the proposed quota system to be imposed on the Hawaiian sugar planters -- Hawaii can produce less high grade sugar and California will get more of its raw sugar from other sources and pay

Hawaii more -- but all I hear is that the planters here want none of the deal.

My anxieties about traveling with this woman seem ridiculous now, though the propriety of it is still in question, to my mind, at least. Often she pauses to point out a bird wearing an extravagance of tropical plumage or a waterfall tucked into a cleft of moss-covered rock. She is a good guide, & most capable horsewoman, going along with undulant ease on a trail that vacillates, first this way up the mountain, then switching back down toward the brink where the surf crashes below us -- "makai" she tells me - toward the sea. Were it not for the mane and sturdy ears of my mount to use as handles, I would have been unseated a good many times. The back of me remembers well the consequences of such a ride on Oahu and is grateful that this is a more languid pace - and that my backside has toughened somewhat. It's easy to see why the natives don't make this trip by land often - they resort to water rather than clamber up these crevices and down again. We didn't meet a single traveler all day.

Though I prefer mules, our horses move nimbly along this trail. They are a black and a tan, "Nigger" and "Boy" by name, acquired from a haole willing to rent the saddles and horseflesh to go under them. I mostly followed along on my sturdy mare, watching the woman's brown shoulders above the wrap of cloth she wears as she trots along, gripping her tan mount with her knees like a man, foregoing the maidenly convention of sidesaddle. With this morning's setting out she has stashed the dull calico dress of the missionary style and wears a length of material wrapped ingeniously - and with apparent security - about her in the native way, covering her from just below her shoulders to the knee more or less, and generally less.

We camped for the night and from nowhere but the calabashes and forest Napua produced an evening meal that - my ravenous hunger notwithstanding - rivaled any repast offered me since leaving Honolulu. There is abundant food all around us, if you know what to look for. The Hawaiian language has no word for time *but a dictionary's worth for eating! Hunger is their idea of Hell. Napua has gathered breadfruit (oo-loo) and guava and passion fruit to add to the provisions we carried along. We share the simple fare of a campfire - yams, papaya, dried up poi, and fish, and a stewed chicken, tough as sinew, though the papaya she had cooked with it took some of the characteristic rigor out of the old hen. I remarked that it was probably one of those chickens that had come from Cook - she did not smile, having the same disdain for the Discoverer that most of her kind seem to harbor & with good reason. My remark that however old it might have been, it certainly did come from the cook and well-done too did not bring a laugh either. It is hard working a turn of phrase on these Kanaka - they don't seem to appreciate it. I valiantly tried to entertain my hostess with a version of the jumping frog story, but she was unacquainted with those critters, there being none of any stature or consequence in these islands.*

I begin to itch for conversation, as I did when marooned in New York, but for more pleasant reasons. There the jumbled pace of the city prevents palaver while here it is the missionary bent of my companion that renders her sedately silent and me lonesome for campfire chat.

Very early, Emily woke the next morning as she always did, alert, slightly anxious, immediately wondering what day it was and what work there was to do. There was a subtle easing in her belly as she remembered where she was and that she did not have to go to the campus today and wade their pools of academic angst. It was a relief to be caught up in the comfortable solitude of research - until she saw the leather journal where she had carefully laid it the night before.

She reached for it, feeling again the vague familiarity that had seeped into her last night, as if the writer was someone she had known, perhaps a voice she had heard, an echo of some forgotten story. The cover felt warm in her hands as she opened the journal to where she had left off. The scent of maile drifted up to her again and the memory of Kamuela with it. Kamuela - his warmth, his hair pulled into a knot at the back of his head, his hazel eyes - she almost felt his presence in the room. He had known that the old book would intrigue her. It seemed to be a travel diary by some 19th century visitor to the islands, and because it was a man's rather than some undiscovered woman's, and not Melville's, it would have had little interest for her professionally. But the lingering sense that she was somehow acquainted with the writer, that she nearly recognized his voice, would have kept her reading had it not been for the appointment she had this morning with the historian at the community college. She slipped the antique notebook into her bag.

It was plain to Emily why people rose early in Hawaii. This morning, as every morning, shimmered. Every rock, tree, wave and blossom wore its aura. The day's heat was only hinted at in the warmth of the wind as she stepped out into the air from the old professor's office. There had been the expected professional courtesies mingled with some delight on his part that she had come so far to ask him her questions about Melville, but in the end, there was neither news nor confirmation about the material she sought. She shrugged her bag onto her shoulder, surprised somewhat at her lack of disappointment, and paused on the grass to consider the situation.

There across the lawn, among the trees, a shadow shifted into Kamuela's shape, lounging against the thick trunk of a plumeria tree, a white flower tucked over his right ear. She did not look at him as they moved toward each other.

He made it easy for her again. “Aloha. It is a beautiful day for swimming. Will you come?”

“How did you find me?”

He nodded toward the rental car for answer. “Would you like to go for a swim? I could drive.” He tilted his head toward a small blue Toyota parked further down the curb, rusted and ragged with a ti leaf lei hanging from the rearview mirror and the snout of a surfboard poking out a back window.

“Where? Is it far?”

“Not far.”

“I could follow you in my car.” Or you could ride with me, she nearly said.

He shrugged. “Your car might have trouble with the road. It is not made for rentals.”

The prospect of going to some remote off-road beach with this virtual stranger should have made her wary - and would have back in New York - but Kamuela’s steadfast ease and gentleness, coupled with the mystery of his eyes, soothed any anxiety, and she assented. He shouldered her purse while she grabbed her leather satchel from her car, putting them in the back seat next to a cooler and the surfboard. When he opened the car door for her to get in, its grind and squeal made her hesitate. She noticed that the seat was newly covered in a cloth of tapa design that mimicked the layers of material that he had wrapped the journal in.

It was his quiet that eased her. Used to the incessant conversation of professional men back in Buffalo - and all of it about themselves and their work - she found it comfortable to bump along and look about her without the necessity of making appropriate comments in response to some self-reflexive litany. Instead, the silence between them let her look at Hawaii around her and take it in without having to do anything or even think about it.

She recognized the road he turned onto as one that the rental car maps had marked off limits, with good reason, she thought, as Kamuela negotiated deep holes filled with rock and rainwater. Slowly they bumped their way toward a stand of kiawe trees and surf. The road made a quick bend that Kamuela expertly kept to the outside of just as a rusty jeep came at them, driving too fast, tires spewing stones and tearing up the old beach road even more. The load of local boys, dark-eyed and territorial, responded respectfully to his wave and nod and waited until the blue Toyota had moved on toward the beach before they drove on more slowly themselves. Emily understood that she had been seen and dismissed only because she was with Kamuela in this obviously local car.

The rubble and red earth turned to sand just inside the trees, and he parked in shade where they could look over a narrow crescent beach, a pale quarter moon of sand that embraced gentle water. Further out, the surf broke against a reef, and it was that roiling water that Kamuela studied. Wordlessly, he carried their gear to a patch of shade, spreading sweet-smelling grass mats and anchoring them with the cooler.

The sun was hot where it hit her, but the wind in the trees shifted the light and played disconcertingly with the feel of summer on her skin, chiaroscuro of bright heat and shaded coolness.

"Swim now?" he asked. She nodded. "Do you have a suit?"

"Of course." She looked for a bathhouse to change in, but this was a local beach and had none of those amenities that the counties put out for tourists. Kamuela nodded toward a clump of heliotrope that would provide some privacy.

"I'll just go into the water and wait for you." He peeled out of his t-shirt and sauntered to the water's edge. She dug her swimsuit out of her bag, a bit smug that she was the sort of woman who had every contingency covered.

In the shallows, the water was remarkably warmer than she had expected, bath-like. She slipped in and stroked out deeper toward Kamuela. He moved through the water with dolphin ease that was surprising in a man as broad and solid as he was. As he slid past her, the shadow of a long tattoo over his shoulder caught her eye. When he broke the surface again, she avoided his eyes by looking carefully at the tattoo, a band of blue-black geometrics that ran over his shoulder and down his chest on the right side. Beneath the surface, she glimpsed the same design tracing the ridge of his thigh and disappearing under the edge of his swim trunks. She spun in the water, swimming out toward the break, away from him, slicing through the sea powerfully and a little proudly. Swimming was one of the things she did well. Summers at the lake and then the long hours of mindless swimming in the college pool had given her grace and stamina in the water. When she was out deep enough, she dove in smooth arcs, her pale body more so against the black tank suit, until she was a dappled blur in the aquamarine.

He let her be and returned to the beach, laying out the lunch he had packed for them early that morning feeling more than hopeful that he would find her willing to go with him. When she was tired, she floated in and pulled herself up from the shallows, shaking the water from her hair as she went. He met her with a jug of fresh water and splashed it over her to get some of the salt off before they spread themselves on the mats.

He watched her pleasure and smiled broadly. She tugged at the top of her suit needlessly and shifted on the mat, finally pulling her towel around her.

"Hungry?"

"Actually, I am!" She seemed surprised.

"Good. We have . . . " and he recited the menu he'd packed, touching each dish with reverence as if it was an offering, "and poi. I thought you would like poi, perhaps."

"I've never tasted it." She already knew about poi's reputation with tourists. She took the spoon he held out to her, drawing the smooth paste onto her tongue, tasting the faint fermented taint that gave poi its full flavor. Delicious, in its way. She smiled delightedly at him and they began to talk at last, as they ate, easy in the shared pleasure of a picnic. They spoke of the water, and she asked too many questions. When he had named the trees and birds and explained the surf break, she asked him about himself.

"And you work at the church?" She had devoutly hoped that he wasn't a minister or deacon or something like that.

"Part-time. I am the docent there. I teach too - at the Community College - Hawaiian language classes mostly. The Hawaiian studies program itself isn't fully developed or funded yet, but we offer as many classes as we can - chants, language, history."

She realized he had slipped out of the elliptical speech of the shaman and spoke now in the familiar cadences of the well educated. Kamehameha School, perhaps, and then the University of Hawaii? She guessed correctly, and for a time diverted his attention from herself while he talked about teaching, his family, and the islands. He spoke of the years of graduate school in Oregon as if they had been a time of exile or imprisonment, but clearly it had prepared him well to return and "take my place to help our people," as he said. He only alluded to his later studies over on the Big Island with the *kahuna*, leaving her to guess at what arcane practices might have been added to his education there. The lilt in his voice carried his precise words revealing the heritage of the ancient islands while he explained that these days there was little paid work for anyone who was adept in the old arts, so he had pieced together a series of jobs that suited his talents and beliefs. "It's a hard life here. Nearly everyone works at two jobs to support the ohana - the family. The ones who can't work take care of the land and the children." He asked her nothing about herself, waiting. She volunteered nothing. His gaze penetrated her reserve, and she shifted, conscious again of her skin where it was warmer than the chill of her wet swimsuit.

"Have you looked into the notebook?" he asked. It was the only safe subject. He was making it easy for her again by not asking her about herself.

"Yes. It seems familiar somehow." She reached into her bag for it, leaning past him and feeling his warmth where she was cool. She had wrapped the notebook carefully in a plastic laundry bag she'd found in the motel bathroom and wanted him to see that she was keeping it safe. She wondered how much and what to tell him. Travel writing was usually about ego rather than environment, description not diatribe, but in this journal there seemed to be some tension between the selves of the traveler and writer, some resistance, as if the writer wanted to tell a different story than this one, something deeper he needed to hide from his readers – or himself. "It's unusual as travel diaries of that period go."

He nodded and drew breath the way she had noticed before, a pause before he said something important. "Every person makes two journeys in a lifetime. The outer one has mileposts, incidents, schedules and luggage. The inner voyage has its own secret history and baggage."

Emily was unsure whether that pronouncement was about the journal or her or both. "Yes, well—I'd like to keep it awhile, if you don't mind."

"Of course. As long as you like."

"Have you read it yourself?" He nodded assent, offering her nothing more than that.

The afternoon hummed around them. Emily recognized a familiar impulse in herself. A moment had passed, and she was at some kind of intersection, a pause, and normally she would withdraw now, pull back, go home alone, rather than wait for what was next, the thing she didn't know. It was why she always drove her own car to a party, so she could leave when this moment came on her and she would hurry away to get on to the next thing or go back to work rather than be suspended in the moment of transition to whatever new feeling might come. This time, there was no way to escape.

He saw her impulse to bolt and knew she needed a bit of space.

"I think I will surf now. Do you mind? Perhaps you would like to swim again?"

"I don't know. You go ahead."

He went into the water without looking back at her, knowing she watched him. When she could no longer see the dark tattoo on his shoulder, she lay back against the fragrant grass mat, cradled the book on her chest and fell into a drowse. She could hear the pulse in her ears, it was so quiet. In all the years she had spent alone in archives and libraries, she had never heard such quiet or the rush of her blood within her. Only the diary slipping to the mat roused her from the shimmering. She began to read again.

April 16

I write this not knowing if it will ever find its way to a reader. We have nearly perished in a storm, a veritable avalanche of rain, a flood, a torrent. We were making our way slowly toward Hana and the residence of the good reverend there whose name I have quite forgotten, when Napua began to look anxiously at the sky and held her face into the strengthening wind as if taking the scent of it. It wasn't long before she halted our ambling steeds and pointed northward - or east perhaps - and I saw a tumult of ominous clouds hurtling toward us. Beneath them, rain streaked into the sea, driven nearly horizontal by the winds behind. Napua urged me to hasten on a bit to the home of some Christian folk she knew of, but between us and them there was a gulch of considerable depth, though not wide. We pressed ahead, leading the animals to make haste, but before we had gone a quarter mile, the storm overtook us. An extravagance of Nature! Noah would have recognized it. Within moments we were wet to our skins - which isn't saying much about Napua, dressed as she was in the simple sarong of her custom. Napua dripped. The cloth of her wrapped garment clung to her in a way that made the rain a blessing, while I was cloaked in that damnable duster with my lauhala hat providing a sort of umbrella and boots that seemed to invite the water into that space between the sole and upper so that I squished with every step. But these irritations were nothing to me in the next moments.

Just as we began the descent into that gulch, there was a rushing above us, and then a roar and a surge of raging water the color of ale burst over a rock ledge at the head of the declivity and ripped down the green sward in front of us not more than eight feet below. It was then Napua saved my life, pulling me upward over a tangle of vine and creepers, over boulders and moss until she had hauled the horse and me to a glade densely covered over with canopy. Had our horses moved a bit faster, we'd have been caught there in the bottom of the gorge and washed away to sea.

But we stood cut off from the path in front of us by this new river, surrounded by brawling water, suspended in it. The memory of that $2 fortune teller in New Orleans insinuated itself between my fear and relief. Napua seems to have out-maneuvered my fate and thwarted the seer's prediction that this year would be a dangerous one for me around moving water!

It's here I sit writing this adventure, here in the relative safety of the light of a brisk fire my good guide has made. We've taken refuge in a sort of woodsman's lean-to, open on one side, cobbled primarily of bamboo. Napua has gathered fronds of various sorts and woven a cover for the front side to keep out the rain, and it's not altogether unpleasant with a little fire drying us out. I wish we had a door to shut to keep out the wet world and hold in the cozy. All around us is water, much of it with the fragrance faintly like the wet-earth smell of the Mississippi – perfume of compost and dead vegetation and deceased men's remains, heavier than air. Now and then the sea wind breaks in with freshness. My rucksack upturned in the exertions of the rescue and I lost a few cigars as well as my watch, the pricey one the boys gave me in Nevada for being the lead malcontent. I shall miss the cigars. Good fortune prevailed and the whiskey I carried along in the saddlebag was saved and now has quite warmed my blood. The woman refuses any such comfort. Must be the missionary in her.

Samuel sat in the center of the shelter, his coat and shirt strung up behind him to dry. He had resisted, at first, her insistence on his stripping off his clothes rather than sitting in them. It offended his modesty - or perhaps his vanity - to be exposed thus, and she had tossed a length of dry cloth over his naked shoulders when she saw his blush under the burn and blister on his cheek. Around them, the trees moaned in the wind and the stalks of bamboo strained and creaked where they were lashed together to make this retreat. Everywhere was the sound of water, the steady drip of rain from the forest canopy above them, the further off thudding raindrops on the leaf-cushioned forest floor in front of the lean-to, and farther yet the rush of water in the gulch that had almost claimed them.

But it was quiet when he awoke. Napua lay in an easy curl near his feet. She slept deeply, it seemed, as he looked without fear of offending her. She was, he saw now, softer in the face than he had first thought, being of that class of Hawaiians who had lost - or perhaps never had - that coarseness of feature one saw in the visages of the horse dealers, stevedores and whores in Honolulu. Her skin, in the dim light, was darker than cinnamon, and looked as if it would have the smooth welcome of velvet if he touched her. She wore again the calico tent the missionaries prescribed, but the fact of her body as he had seen it in the rain bore down on him. There was something in the angle of her cheek and curve of hip that roused him, and he drew back from a thought. It was all well and good to banter about the half-naked charms of the dusky beauties on the streets of Honolulu, but this Napua lay before him too real to think about in that way.

She opened her eyes and looked back at him. In the half-dark, he could not be sure she was awake and hesitated to speak. She stretched out of the languor of her sleep with grace and not a bit of self-consciousness.

"Sleeping Beauty," he muttered.

"Say again?"

"Nothing. It's time to go, I suppose. We should be moving on." He had only allotted a week for Maui and the study of the sugar industry, and now four days of it were gone, and he reckoned they were still a day's journey from their destination at the Rev. Mr. Finn's in Hana.

"The rain is less, but the streams will still be rivers. We will wait."

"How long?"

"Tomorrow." She shrugged in a small way. "The next day."

"But they will be waiting for us in Hana."

"They will know."

The old eagerness to be in motion, on the way to somewhere, tugged at him, but the scent of greenery and the limpid light around him exerted its own pull, and he gave in to lassitude. Another cigar seemed in order, and he drew one from his diminished cache. His journal lay closed beside him on the floor. Time enough for that later, he thought. He rose, drawing the cloth around him like a shawl, and stepped out through the fringe of palm Napua had left like a doorway, his bare feet slipping on the sodden fronds and branches that formed the floor of their refuge. Looking past the edge of it, he was startled to see water rushing beneath the place where he stood. The whole mountain was awash, and he was perched in the middle of a river of rainwater that ran underneath their forest haven. Except for there being no motion, it was like riding a boat down some slant current. He turned inside again thinking of a raft tethered to the mountainside against the rage of rain and knowing that he was not the pilot of this vessel, this trip.

April 18

There are only two seasons in Hawai'i – dry summer and wet.

Two days of relentless rain, but I'd have endured forty such days of gloom and terror for the glory that greeted me when the rain ended and we stepped out into the night. The moon had risen and hung there almost directly above our heads, flooding the mountainside and ocean with silver light. Mahealani - Napua calls it. (ma-hay-a-la-knee) Its brilliance dimmed the stars around it somewhat, but that seemed no loss when weighed against the dazzle of the moonlight. It wasn't just the beauty of the moon that stirred me but the fact of it. A fortnight ago I rode out to Waikiki braced to observe the total eclipse of that waning arc and saw it disappear, leaving nothing but the surrounding gems suspended in a darkness as deep as the ocean before us. It makes a civilized man consider the pagan perspective about these celestial matters to see it go, leaving him without any point of reference in the dark, and then, with none of his doing, coming again to light the night as it does now.

The sky here is closer to earth than anywhere else.

The sky above the next island to the south - Hawai'i island - is lit with Pele's fire, dimming the stars above it. I am eager to see Kilauea where the eruptions go on unabated. I proposed to Napua that she go on to that island with me, but she demurs. She is a fine guide & companion. I will be sorry when my time here is done.

Tonight, gazing toward California, I endeavored to tell her about the West but was confounded by the uncertainty of my internal compass. I suppose I was looking eastward,, though I'm not at all sure of the direction. The moss grows all the way around the trees here, not just on the north side, and I have lost all contact with the cardinal points completely, knowing only where the sun sets and rises but otherwise suspecting we are adrift in a watery universe that requires only the two directions Kanakas use - makai for toward the sea and mauka for toward the mountain. I am uncertain as wild birds are, not knowing where they are but yet not lost. Looking makai, I catch the black edge of rain clouds moving away from us, unveiling the dazzling sky like a widow doffing her weeds. It is the same with me. I have given up the struggle against the old gloom and melancholy that have haunted me. They hold no power against the languid pleasures and delightful surprises of this paradise.

Here I find the same delight that Adam must have savored - of seeming to be the First Man, seeing what none has seen before, putting one's foot down where there is no path, no print of previous inhabitants or travelers. An ecstasy of freshness. More American than the western frontier is this island Eden, with large still-untrammeled portions where a man - and woman - might find a glade and set up rude housekeeping before a waterfall that white men have never seen. America has begun to acquire the trappings of the Old World - relics, ruins, legends, history, and wars to wax nostalgic over. This little kingdom likewise has its History of Man, and each day surrenders bits of its Garden innocence to the ravishment of civilization, but there are yet to be found here vast valleys and swathes of mountain where a man can be Adam again, or Columbus! Here a man like myself is neither prince nor pauper but both, living in freedom from want and the poor's imperative to work to survive.

My guide and companion Napua is a creature of a different sort from the comely, frolicsome innocents I have observed in Honolulu's byways. The city's Kanaka girls are much like the ladies on steamboats back on the big river, generous and elastic in their morality, though the island variety is more naïve and decidedly more beautiful than river women and hurdy-gurdy girls. Napua is more sedate and genteel than Honolulu girls, no doubt the fault of her missionary upbringing. Yet she seems to have benefited from the license of these Episcopalians the king has established at his court! She has left off her Christian pieties with her calico, and her pidgin lends piquancy to any conversation. In her the spareness of New England protestantism has got a good grip on native exuberance with the result that even as she walks about barefoot and half-peeled, there is an air of queenly grace about her. A perfect Christian savage. She's full of reserve and resolution, with a degree of dignity such as I have often found in the wisest folk I have known. Thanks to the missionaries, the Hawaiians are the most literate people on the planet, by the numbers. Unlike the colored and Indians and rural ruffians, every Sandwich Islander goes to school. By the age of ten, every child can read and write English. Napua went to the girls' school in Lahaina - one of the few respectable buildings in that town. It used to be the Seaman's Hospital, built by the previous King Kamehameha (with a more or less willing warrior buried in the NE corner for luck). Her reading has been regulated by the clerics to only the most chaste, her mental and physical daintiness thereby assured.

Napua - the flowers, it means in her language. She was named before birth – and not by her parents – in the Kanaka way. Napua. But that's not the whole of it! Like all these folk, royal and common alike, she's got a mile-long name brimful of vowels and pauses but very little real breathing space. There's likely an aloha in there somewhere too, it seems, and she has a Christian name as well - Sarah - though she eschews the rule imposed by the missionaries that everyone have both a pagan and a protestant name. She carries a sheaf of papers and pencil in her bundle, and I have caught her quietly writing sometimes when I wake. Like her evening prayers, it seems to be a part of her daily discipline - surprising now that she appears to have left behind the trappings of her missionary education when she stashed the calico dress and put on the garb of her people. There is a stunning smile and heart-free girl's laugh in her, when she forgets or forgives my haole presence. She laughs at me a good deal more than is warranted, I think, but I am willing to provide merriment for her. At least she doesn't try to civilize me - lets me smoke as much as I like and wherever I care to, the first time I have had such liberty since I adopted the vice.

April 19

Napua is a study in the quiet that these island people have so perfected. She never speaks unless she can improve the silence. Kanaka are not much for storytelling, unlike colored folk. They have an aversion to chatter but will sit all day in quiet camaraderie with you. It takes awhile for one such as myself to appreciate terse Hawaiian eloquence and rhetorical silences. Napua hardly talks unless I put a direct question to her, but she's an apt listener - to birdsong and wind and every stirring, including my chatter. Never asks a question. Seems not to have the least curiosity about anything beyond what she knows - this place and the people who live here. Not inquisitive about America - or me - though she's an avid audience for my talk at night. How insular they are, these island folk, with little interest or none in anything beyond the horizon before them and the green mantled mountain behind. What breeds such sweet contentment?

Since I first embarked upon my westering sojourn - no, even before that - since first I went upon the Mississippi - I have kept an eye always on the horizon and wanted only to be there, wherever I wasn't. Then I would arrive there and find that there wasn't any there there, no place with a heart to it, only another port or crossroads, and the eagerness to be off again would catch me up. I have always been driven with an impulse to see and know where it was that I was not. My own itch for seeing the back side of everywhere is as alien to

Kanaka as maple syrup.

What gives the piquancy to travel is fear – being far from what's familiar – the traveler feels an ancient and instinctual fear surge up and insist that he scurry back to old habits and sights. In going on a trip, we quiver at the edge of newness, yet we tramp about, looking behind to see the old home as if it was now a foreign land, with its warts as well as wonders. Along the way, as hours and miles ricochet off memory and anticipation, a man checks his internal weather and gauges the climate and finds that the old land wasn't so comfortable – merely familiar.

"Lahaina" means a particular variety of sugarcane, they say, and there's considerable sign of that industry's excesses and successes as well as the residue of whalermen's debauchery and dereliction. Generally the old place has an air of the wild west about it, with seamen instead of cowboys and prospectors, of course, but that same tolerance for roughnecks and eccentrics that a man finds in the friendliest towns in Nevada and California and along the Mississippi River. Compared to Lahaina, Wailuku is a two horse town, having taken precedence since the whaling trade has fallen off leaving Lahaina with its frayed collars and shabby soles (souls!) showing.

In the dusk, Napua called out to me to come to supper - "Mr. Clemens!" - and I prevailed upon her to call me Samuel. Like the good Christian girl she was reared to be, she recognized that fine Old Testament cognomen at once and commenced a short discourse on my namesake - the first of the prophets, saint and seer, a list of attributes that made me downright uncomfortable, to tell the truth. "Kamuela" - she says it the Hawaiian way, without the hiss in it. A frown ensued across that dusky brow. Perhaps she didn't think the name was a good fit. "Mark Twain" required a good deal of explaining - to no avail - the frown remaining. "We shall have to find you a right Hawaiian name," she said, and it is a baptism I anticipate with some delight!

Emily studied the handwriting again. Clemens. That is clearly what it said. And Mark Twain. Samuel. The initials on the letter - SLC - Samuel Langhorne Clemens?

Spring-tight, Emily struggled with what to do next. Kamuela was out there beyond reach. She couldn't take the car and go, but she needed to get to a library. She needed to be sure, to know what it was that she held - a hoax? or a piece of undiscovered Twainiana, a vein of gold in the scholarly industry that had grown up around Mark Twain and his work?

Unable merely to sit and wait or even keep reading, she gathered their things, cleaned the remains of the picnic, dressed again and perched on a stone watching for Kamuela, holding the journal. When he strolled across the narrow beach at last, he drew back from the tension in her face, looking instead at the journal between them.

"Why didn't you tell me?" her voice as edgy as she felt.

"Would you have believed?" He had her there.

"I need to go. I have to get to a library, check the facts."

"Tomorrow."

"No. I must know."

"You already know."

"Maybe."

He shrugged, and his shoulders slumped with disappointment.

"I have to know." She would not ask him, not yet, how he came to have it or why he chose her to give it to. Facts first. She asked about the campus library hours and holdings, and after that they didn't talk as he drove her back to the campus. Along the way he glanced at her and smiled but did not talk at all. Her old habits of concentration were spurred by the lure of a literary "find" and yet sorely tested by the tug of Kamuela so close by. Even though the library was already closed for the day and there was no other reason to hurry, she got out of his car before he had time to open the door for her. She stood anxious and a little unsteady as he handed over her bags. This time, she would have to be the one to ask.

"Would you like to - could I - could we have dinner? Tomorrow?"

He leaned toward her and laid his cheek along hers. "Tomorrow." As easy as that. By the time she sat behind the wheel again, the warmth where he had touched her was gone.

Back in her room at The Islander, Emily didn't take time to even undress, but only sluiced cold water over her face and dug the paperback out of the deep pocket of her bag for a cursory look at the copy of Twain's Sandwich Island dispatches she had picked up at the airport. The introduction and scholarly notes were somewhat useful. It was second-hand research, not the kind of impeccable sleuthing that scholarly work demanded, but it placed Twain in Hawai'i at the right time and concluded with a tantalizing comment from his published articles, which he called his "letters," to the Sacramento Union newspaper. The dispatch dated May 23, 1866, was mostly about the Hawaiian legislature, and concluded:

"It has been six weeks since I touched a pen. In explanation and excuse I offer the fact that I spent that time (with the exception of one week) on the island of Maui. I only got back yesterday . . . I never spent so pleasant a month before, or bade any place good-bye so regretfully. . . I went to Maui to stay a week and remained five. I had a jolly time. I would not have fooled away any of it writing letters under any consideration whatever. It will be five or six weeks before I write again. I sail for the island of Hawaii tomorrow, and my Maui notes will not be written up until I come back."

Where were the "Maui notes"? Scholars knew that Twain was prodigious in his journal note-taking and that not having a cache of details, facts, figures, names, seeds of ideas for stories, pronunciations – not having kept a notebook during those weeks on Maui - would be more than uncharacteristic. It would be a lie. Yet there was also a reference to a message written to his sister Mollie as he returned from Maui on May 22, 1866 where he had said "I have not written a single line and have not once thought of business or care or human toil or trouble or sorrow or weariness."

Excitement amped Emily's consciousness, and she remembered reading about the recent discovery of a cache of correspondence from the aged Twain, a discovery that had reconstructed scholars' image of the old man as a depressed cynic. The box of letters had surfaced in an attic on Long Island, of all places. Her discovery of this journal was no more unlikely. Early biographers of Twain had neutralized and neutered the rascal writer, sanitizing his image to fit the white broadcloth suits he favored later in his life. Perhaps she now held a means of replacing some of that reverence with reality. There was still a year to go before Twain's last autobiography could be made public. He had decreed that it would have to be kept under wrap until he had been dead one hundred years. To find an authentic original now that would ignite a re-reading of the young Twain's work would be a scholar's coup, the kind of thing that makes a career, for a while at least. The timing of this was either uncanny good luck or some cosmic fulfillment of prophecy, as Kamuela seemed to be telling her.

She had the direction for tomorrow's research, but

there was little to be done that evening, and Emily submitted to the lure of the sunset, ambling downtown for some supper and ending up at the seawall. The sound of rowdies at the bar in the Pioneer Inn urged her along Front Street to a place where tourists lingered before dinner at one of the little restaurants nearby. She wasn't hungry. When the sun had dropped behind the horizon, without the much-touted green flash, she headed back, resolute about an early night.

But the sheets rasped against her skin where the sun had touched her. She felt the planes of her body chilled and then hot against the night, sensitive to every nuance of breeze across her. It was too much like other nights alone in bed, body-conscious and hungering and hating it. As much as she wanted to sleep, and as hard as she tried to be still and will it, the old restlessness came on her instead. Night sounds swirled around her and the insistent scent of frangipani seeped through the jalousies like a call to waken. She turned on the light and picked up the journal again, but before she began to read, the phone beside her bed rang for the first time since she had arrived in Hawai'i. There was no one back there in Buffalo or anywhere else in America who would be checking-in with her or just calling to chat. Probably it was the switchboard ringing the wrong room, she thought, but it rang again insistently.

"Yes?" she answered crisply, sure it was a mistake.

"Are you reading?" Kamuela's voice came quietly, very near, as if he whispered to her across the bed.

"No - yes. I was trying to." *I can't sleep* seemed too

much to reveal.

"Aloe - try aloe for the sunburn." He said it "alo-ay" in the Hawaiian way the first time. "I put a bottle into your bag back at the beach."

"Thank you." She wanted to say more but could not think of what it should be or could be.

"Well --- good night." His voice telegraphed intimacy the way his warmth did.

"Wait! Tomorrow. Dinner, remember?" she sounded a bit urgent even to herself.

"I would not forget. Good night."

The air in the small campus library was sterile and chilled as Emily pushed inside. The dimmed light and cold quiet was familiar, and she felt the switches in her mind clicking even faster than they had all night. Behind the information desk, a tall Hawaiian woman rose to meet her, majestic as a mountain rising from mist, her calico *mu'umu'u* unfolding around her. She was not smiling, but Emily recognized the cascade of pewter hair and black eyes, the elegant ease and fluid grace of the woman who had shared the plane ride from Chicago with her.

"Hello!" Emily was not sure the woman remembered her. "What a surprise to see you again!"

There was little response except a stiffening of the older woman's shoulders and a slight sway in the folds of her dress. "Well, it *is* an island. How may I help you?"

Emily felt the rebuff and retreated into professional mode. "I am professor Emily Witt, University at Buffalo." The familiar sense of being an impostor nudged her. She was always slightly annoyed by the feeling that her working-class roots would somehow be obvious and reveal her life as a professor at a good public university to be a pose, somehow fraudulent. "I am looking for information on Mark Twain, Samuel Langhorne Clemens, and I need access to the holdings at the University of Hawai'i at Manoa. Is that possible?" Emily fumbled for her faculty ID, tugging it up from the bottom of the bag, displacing the journal so it thudded out onto the counter between them. The older woman looked hard at it and sighed.

"So. He found you. And he gave it to you," she murmured, as much to herself as to Emily. "Kamuela. My nephew. I am Malia Keana'aina, his mother's sister." She picked up the journal in its plastic covering and held it as if it were dangerous or dirty. "When I saw you on the plane, I thought it might be you. He dreamed you were coming." There was the same lilting voice as Kamuela's but an inclement edge underneath it.

Emily found her voice. "You know about the journal?"

"Of course. It has always been kept safe by our *ohana*," she paused, assuming this young scholar would not know the word or its importance, "our family. Kamuela has had it many years. My mother gave it to him rather than to me or my sister, thinking he would know best how to keep it. None of us ever intended for anyone else to see it. No one outside the *ohana*. But Kamuela dreamed, and he was sure." She gestured helplessness.

"It appears to be a travel diary written by Mark Twain. I need to check some information before I can be sure."

"Sure of what?"

"That is it authentic."

"Why?"

"If it is, it would be an important new piece of Twain material. It might revise everything we know about the early Twain. Scholars will be clamoring for its publication."

"No."

"No?"

"It must not be published. We cannot allow that." Emily scarcely understood what she clearly heard. "The *ohana* will not allow it. Kamuela - he never should have let you see it. It was better that it remain a secret."

"But it is - or it might be - such a significant find for scholars! You don't intend to keep it hidden forever, do you?"

"If it was <u>your</u> family" - Malia bent to look at the faculty ID card that Emily still held out to her - "Professor Witt - if it was your family, would you publish it for all the world to read?"

It was a question Emily could not understand, alien to her own system of what was fair game for scholars and journalists, and invested as was she in the hope that this would be the find of her career. "But - it's Mark

Twain! You must see how important it is!"

"I see how important it is to you, but you do not understand what it means to us. We do not broadcast our family's shame, even if it was some famous *haole*. We are proud people, proud to be Hawaiian. We do not want to be part of some *haole* family's history."

Emily held fast to the journal, half afraid the elder woman would wrest it away from her, but Malia merely looked into the scholar's eyes. Emily wondered if in fact the family really would stop her from publishing it, if it proved legitimate, and if there was any appeal she could make to them. If the public glare of notoriety was the issue, would money trump their pride?

There was ice in the air as Malia turned and swept away like a brig under sail. Emily spotted the library computers and dropped her bag beside one, sliding the journal deep inside for safekeeping. An hour later, she had located the journals of Mark Twain in the stacks - an unlikely piece of good luck, she knew - and read enough of the introduction to know that probably she had an authentic artifact in her bag. Amidst the scholarly confusion about dates of entries in his journals was the first confirmation she needed: Mark Twain had alternated writing in what were now called Notebook 5 and Notebook 6, but scholars believed that between those two there was another notebook, a missing journal, containing his notes of his travels on Maui. There was a gap of eight weeks between his time on Oahu and his return from the Big Island of Hawaii, an interval that included more than a month on Maui. The notebooks on the shelf were scholarly editions in print, not fascimiles of the original handwritten ones, so there was still the unsettling issue of the handwriting. That would have to be sussed out, but if the penmanship in the journal she held matched the originals of the other notebooks in the archives in California, she had enough evidence to proceed. If the pencil scribbles corresponded in style, it would still require meticulous examination through cryptography, graphology and such, but the journal itself was the same sort that 5 and 6 were – leather bound, gilt-edged, in pencil. An industry's arsenal of literary tests would tell her what she already knew intuitively: it was not a hoax.

Kamuela had handed her Mark Twain's lost journal.

When she returned to the main desk, Malia was gone, and in her place a thin Japanese woman wearing enormous glasses perched resolutely behind the sign that read "Kokua" and in smaller letters below, "help." Emily produced the forms to request a few of the newest books and articles on Twain from the central university library on Oahu and hoped that professional courtesy would extend to her here. When she asked for Malia, the sparrow said she did not know, that this was *her* station, that Malia worked elsewhere and maybe the professor could find her there. It was clear to Emily that she had already asked enough, and she adopted an unfamiliar humility in thanking the bird-woman for her help.

Three days until the books would be here for her. Three days. In the meantime, there were the Sandwich Island letters and the journal. And Kamuela.

April 20

I was washing up this morning beside the stream that had lately been a river. The water has turned to cold crystal again. I felt a twinge of guilt and teaspoonful of remorse remembering my escapade at Waikiki - sitting on the clothes of those naked beauties bathing themselves in the surf. With the shoe off the other foot, it wasn't quite so comical. Napua had taken my clothes away to clean them. Lolling on the bank, I had my reverie and remorse interrupted by a flash of whiteness moving in the trees above me where the water cascaded over a rocky ledge worn smooth by centuries of mountain water. Before I had taken a good draw on my morning cigar, I saw a bundle glide down that first waterfall and disappear into a high up pool before bumping over another outcropping and sliding with the water down a slight incline, past me where I lounged, and into a pool below. It bobbed against the eddies some while I considered what it might be, and then I discerned a pair of feet at one end, a head at the other, and saw that it was a man, still half-clothed in tattered white trousers. When the current rolled him over, I could see his hands tied together in front of him. It was the leper. Whether by some mischance or suicidal design, the Kanaka had gone over the ridge above us and been swept away. He had made good his escape but could not get free of the rope. He chose the certain death of waterfall to being caught again and hauled off to Molokai. Death one way or the other. Before I could think what should be done next, a slight surge in the water pushed his remains over that last rim before the sea and he was gone into the surf below where stream and ocean meet. Napua said it was just as well and let him go, and I felt no impulse to do otherwise. A corpse before breakfast is a sobering sight.

Napua and Samuel had been working at their laundry in the cruelly cold water of the pool. Rain was falling thousands of feet above them where clouds made a ceiling high up the mountain but left them below in dazzling sun. Time and crystal water had all but washed away the presence of the leper. Leaving his trousers piled in safety on the flat rock at the edge, Samuel slipped into the pool while Napua spread his freshly washed things on branches to dry. With a quick vault, she dove into the pool's deepest part, splashing him icily as she passed. For his sake, she still wore her sarong as she swam smoothly toward him where he had begun to shiver in the current. She pulled a small packet of soap from the tucked front of her wrap and gestured her willingness to wash his hair. In need of a barber and conscious of it, he surrendered to her ministrations. She stood behind him, the weight of her body balanced in the flow, and pressed against his back. He felt the warmth of her as her fingers scrubbed his tangle of wild curls, then slowed to a gentle probing.

"Your hair is like the *ehu* people. It has fire in it."

"Ay-hoo? You said that before, but I didn't understand."

"Yes. The *ehu* are the children of Pele, goddess of the volcano. Kilauea is her home. She lived once in Haleakala, but now she is there," she pointed over his shoulder to the next island, Hawai'i. "Pele's children have the fire in their hair like yours."

"That would make me a demi-god. I should like that. We are always on the lookout for ways to elevate ourselves - it is human nature. Where I come from, red-headed folk who rise to a certain status become 'auburn-haired', but being divine? Now that would suit me. I think that I would rather be a child of Pele's than anything. And their eyes? What color are their eyes?"

"Like mine."

Samuel turned his head as she bent around him to look into her eyes, their cheeks colliding, his hot where the sun had burned him. He felt her fingers tighten in his hair before she reached for the gourd to rinse him. She waited while he set his cigar down beside his dry pants, used to the way he always kept one lit when he was still.

"*Pua'ehu,*" she murmured, as much to herself as to him. "Your Hawaiian name should be *Pua'ehu*. It means the one who shines brightly as the red flowers do. "

"Give me a native name, if you please. Christen me!"

"That I cannot do. I am not a missionary. And now the king has made a law that everyone must have a Christian name, the new way."

"What was the old way?"

"You would have a name that came to one of the elders in a dream or a vision, and it would belong to you, and you would become like the name."

"Being named for one's attributes instead of paternity seems liberating, and not so far from 'Mark Twain,' actually. *Pua'ehu.*"

He chewed on the name instead of the cigar, managing to say it finally. She tested it, lingering over the syllables, until delight broke over her face and "Maka alohilohi" burst out of her mouth. "The bright sparkling eyes," she explained. "Maka." That much his tongue could manage, and it was close enough to his pen name to suit him.

Then she poured and rinsed, caressing his head and neck, and finally his shoulders. The suds whirled around them and were washed over the rim of their bathing place. Napua withdrew, and Samuel felt the cold water where her body had been. She climbed easily over the rocks and stepped behind a veil of greenery, untying her sarong as she went, deeply conscious of his gaze as she dropped the dripping garment at just the last instant before she was gone from view, wearing nothing in that moment but sunshine. It seemed like long minutes before he pulled himself over the edge and thanked Almighty God and Pele too for the coldness of the water.

When Emily turned the page of the journal, she saw that one sheet had been imperfectly torn out, leaving a ragged edge and gaping stitches before the scribble resumed on a fresh page.

April ? 23?

My allotted week is more than passed. The schooner is gone back to Honolulu without me, no doubt. It's been more days than I can accurately number since I last put my pencil to work here. Somehow, in the midst of our small store of things, I lost this notebook and have only just now recovered it. I left the earlier one behind in Honolulu, unintentionally but propitiously. It is always good to keep a spare close to hand, but it falls open to more empty pages than I can account for. There's hardly a notation or figure of any sort and nothing at all of the sugar business I was sent to investigate! I am demented with love. Abandoned by my truant wits. The empty pages mock me. What indolence! I'm no better than one of those slack-jawed scalawags one sees about the piers and levees. Exertion seems no virtue. I've taken my ease, alright. And hers. This endless summer and the embrace of paradise have seduced me away from the work.

A human being is naturally inclined to take more of a good thing than he needs.

There was a longer than usual pause on the page, several lines left empty.

I've heard it said that in wild isolation even an ugly woman will look appealing after a month's time. With Napua no such interval is required. She is rather taller than American girls would strive to be, more vigorous, sure-footed, with Amazonian vitality. Her face is aglow with good health that is charming, unlike the parlor prettiness and pale tyranny of American girls. There is no trace of the European in her visage – and she is blessedly endowed with the broad nose of her race. She talks music from that lovely mouth. Her waist is a bit thicker and hips slimmer than the fashion in America. A civilized woman loses half her charm without her dress – some would lose all of it – but not Napua. The first thing the missionaries try to teach the native is indecency, but Nature knows none. Neither does Napua, and in that lies a portion of her charm. The modesty that she wears is the sort that women had before clothes were legislated. Her grace in all things whether cooking or riding or cleaning fish is reason enough to find her lovely, but add to that her dignity, gentleness - refinement, I might say - and a man could not help but find her beautiful despite the darkness of her skin. Even that which would be a blemish on another becomes her, the dusky skin and black eyes having a certain exotic charm and none of the faults of the negro race.

Emily saw that something had been crossed out thoroughly, irretrievably.

In any discussion of the whale trade and the relative merits of San Francisco taking over the whalermen's business for Honolulu and Lahaina, a dozen arguments of commerce are made for why these islands make better ports for whalers, but no one speaks aloud the determining factor - Hawaii's women. What sailor wouldn't sign on to get the guarantee of a layover in paradise and the chance to lay alongside one of its sweet-tempered, warm-bodied and thoroughly lascivious ladies? Say what you might about tariffs and land sharks, telegraph and economics, what Hawaii offers that California cannot is the embrace of its women.

Samuel had moved closer to Napua as she waited, but he halted just shy of reaching for her. The habits of servant girls and California "ladies" were fresh in his memory, but Napua's grace set her apart from any of them he'd bedded. She was not, certainly, one of the demure maidens he'd fixed on back East, genteel and coy, but neither was she a loose and laughing working girl like those he'd known well in his dissipation. She was a being apart who demanded, he was sure, some manner of wooing different from the grope and tumble of the one and the subtle parlor courting of the other. While he had observed the latter, he had never practiced it, and stood now paralyzed by desire and ignorance.

She reached for him. He breathed deeply, like a man surfacing from deep water, and wrapped his arms about her waist as if to hold himself afloat. Napua's hands moved over him, caressing his slight shoulders with a touch like liquid fire through his shirt, pressing him to her until he felt her breasts against him, and then her hips where she urged him, testing his desire, rocking herself until their bodies touched everywhere, until there was no air between them, only heat and urgency. Her hands never stopped the soft rub of love until she stepped back and began to unbutton his shirt.

Her hands brushed the top of his trousers, but she waited, drew back and untied the folds of her sarong, dropping it in the green at their feet. He hardly breathed at the sight of her in the dappled light of the day, standing as her creator had made her. She was the first woman he had seen thus, uncorseted, without chemise or petticoat to hide the sought-for secret places. Napua stood before him without the air of naughty shame that half-garbed girls guarded their sex with. She reigned like Eve before the serpent and the church, erect, proud, shameless, offering more than he could yet imagine, and without guile. Around them, the hum of life in the forest went unnoticed. The shimmering sun penetrated the canopy to cover them in quivering light. Desire urged him, and he began unfastening his trousers. Shame stopped him. The hurried couplings with girls back in America had never required his nakedness, but Napua seemed to insist on it. She held his eyes and saw his unease and found her woman-strength to go to him. Once held, he surrendered to her hands again and they lay naked finally, twining in the half light.

She taught him much. She was more practiced than he in the arts of love and showed him the language of mouth and tongue, the slow withholding, how desire renews itself, the thousand kisses lovers learn, a languorous love that he had never known. The light faded to dusk before they rose and walked, arms draped around each other, sleepy from the afternoon, eager to bathe again and get home to their raft. Once there, the lure of supper faded beside the sweet new desire for each other, and they betook themselves to bed for more delicious fare. A night and day of dear delirium passed before Sam pulled himself out of deep sleep. He had learned much about loving and more of following his own deep instincts and natural inclinations. The rules of right conduct and misdemeanor were joyfully suspended in love with Napua.

She was already moving outside when he awoke and felt the soreness in his muscles from the frolic in the bed. Then he felt her absence. In the first moment of seeing her again, so far beyond arm's reach, she seemed changed to him, more beautiful, softer in her movements. For just a moment, with the impulse to be near her again, came a thought of how he was obliged to her now, what hold she might have over him, what was due and that he had no way to calculate the debt.

April 27

Maui is like a summer Sunday without the sermon and singing. Each day is a lesson in paradise, full of peace and hope with a dash of righteous guilt being the only mar on an otherwise perfect life of toil and repose. Even time doesn't want to pass here.

Wherever Napua is, there is Eden. I am grateful not to be confronted by old Adam's choice of leaving Eden with his Eve or staying without her!

April 28

It is a pleasure to be away from Honolulu's bustle of politics and court intrigues. The royals have adopted the finery and frippery of the English, their court resplendent in velvet and braid. They have discovered that clothes make the man – naked people have little or no influence in politics or society or religion, though half-naked people in rural counties here sometimes do well. Out in the countryside, as it were, the king himself would find his gilded garments unsuitable for an older, harder, more Hawaiian life, the one the majority of his people live. He would do well to go out among the country folk (incognito, of course) to be reminded whom he is responsible to. Had Arthur done it, Victoria might still be holding court at a round table.

The Americans here are too much like democrats at home, publicly mocking royalty and aristocracy but privately hankering after their titles and privileges. Americans adore a foreign government that behaves in ways they would abhor in democratic realms. This monarchy in miniature charms them with its elegant depravity. These days any American father with cash can buy a European title that has a hungry aristocrat attached to add to his family tree. Here haoles who marry into Hawaiian royalty get the land as well as robust, affectionate and lusty mates. It is a far better bargain.

I have cherished even the indifferent Manila cigars that I was able to get in Honolulu and rationed myself accordingly, never smoking more than one at a time and as a general rule saving them for a morning and evening delight. Now Lono, Napua's childhood friend, has procured some good Hawaiian tobacco and a pipe which I find I am enjoying with almost as much relish. The Oahu weed has a fine texture and good flavor, so strong that one cigar satisfies my need for several hours altogether, unlike the Manilas. Lono brings music as well, and sits in the heat of the day or the early darkness playing a bamboo flute - with his nose! It is a curious method, I admit, but it produces music that is better than it sounds, a romantic lilt that wafts around us in the dancing air. It takes considerable skill and no small exertion to continue breathing while exhaling through the nostrils into the long tube, but Napua informs me that Kanaka are used to it, this being the only musical instrument her people had in the time before Capt. Cook. According to their custom, the breath of the mouth might be dangerous, being as it is the source of lies, deceit and intrigue. It was invented after listening to a senator, no doubt. The breath of the nose is always pure, untainted by words, so the sacred music can be safely made.

I would be hard-pressed to tell anyone what this companion of ours looks like. Lono is a perfect shadow, seeming to come and go unexpectedly and almost always just after I have retired to sleep or turned my back for a moment or sneezed. Lono was named after the same god Capt. Cook was mistaken for, but to a better end. Unlike Cook, that ungrateful guest, Lono never overstays his welcome. He is one of those finest fellows, the old style Kanaka, and has proven himself a fast friend to both of us. A sterling character.

From my boy's life in Hannibal I have let my affections cross the line of color to embrace members of the dark race, and I have come to appreciate their fine qualities - warm hearts, loyalty, simplicity, affection, honesty, wisdom. Add to that angelic mix a substantial portion of <u>*Aloha*</u> *and you have a native people here who are good beyond measure, though they will always be horse dealers and maintain all the vices that go with that career and the practice of law, and the women will be lascivious no matter what. All examples of selfishness and greed that whites have shown them have not changed their native generosity any more than examples of white virtue have curbed their licentiousness. Unselfishness and a certain lack of chastity are bred in their blood and bones and will never be civilized out of them, thank goodness.*

In fact, Hawaii could certainly spare the missionaries now. There is more gospel here per capita than anywhere in the world. The missionaries could go home, back to America where there are fields tilled and ready for them to cultivate, especially in Washoe. Besides, the English clerics want the job hereabouts and are slandering the Americans while all the time gobbling up their hard-won converts. The Hawaiians would be safe enough, since the English never get it right anyway.

I would hate to see the Anglicans here impose their Sunday rites upon the natives throughout the kingdom. It seems to me that a religion such as the old Hawaiians had with an assortment of deities and appropriate rituals to propitiate them is preferable to a state religion that is a decreed faith. It is a dangerous thing to regulate a population's faith by establishing a single church as the official one. There is insurance of a sort in having a whole tribe of gods to pick from, protection against the tyranny of the faithful that Americans have with their 40 different Christian creeds and -isms.

A kingdom always models its morals after its monarchs', a rule to which these islands are no exception. The unmarried princess of this kingdom is much celebrated as a woman of appetites, as lusty as any common Kanaka beauty in the realm. These island indians are, like their nobility, barely civilized when it comes to religion, government and bedroom antics. Their brutal ancestry and bloody history is obscured at court by the patina of gold braid and sateen, but their licentiousness remains in public view. Within the royal enclave, the players practice lasciviousness that would get a man shot in Washoe or a woman jailed in Philadelphia. Yet even in the lowest caste there is a gentle humanity. These common natives are generally like children - simple-hearted and slack-brained. But of course brains are hardly necessary – and certainly not desirable - in a society that is based in court and class as a monarchy is. It is a boon to tyranny of the throne that the common natives be dull-witted though educated to literacy. Monarchy is a swindle. A privileged class by "aristocracy" or any other name is but a gang of slaveholders with a title.

There may have been slavery in the dim history of this kingdom - there are rumors of it and Jarves' version of that history alludes to it - but a man was not born or bred into it as the negro was. It was the consequence of warfare, and a man might go from warrior to slave in an afternoon, but it was a risk he took willingly and not because some white man decreed it. There is no caste system in this little kingdom - none of that hierarchy that operates among the members of the colored race in America. Aside from the royal family and alii (ah-lee-ee), the chiefly class and courtiers, the ornamental ranks, no one seems to care much about what degree of native blood one has pulsing in him unless he is intending to stand in line for the throne. Then the Kanaka are ancestor-proud, like southerners. The American rich of NY and Boston can buy shares or marry into a First Family, but being a member of the Ali'i class is more substance than style. One must be bred to it and born with the right ancestors. Otherwise, there is a promiscuous mingling of races and nationalities that has sown a population of robust and beautiful people among whom pedigree matters not at all. There is no one drop rule. Shades of difference seem important only if you are white. In fact, they have a word for anyone who is born from a union between persons of different races - "Hapa" or half. It carries with it, so far as I can see, none of the insult of "mulatto" or "quadroon." Unlike "half-breed" which is applied with such disdain to the Indian in the West, hapa-haole (half-white) or hapa-Hawaiian seems only to serve as a marker for one's heritage, not his race, and as a general thing does not exclude a person from his rights of community and citizenship but unites him in a web of genealogies and shirt-tail relations (called calabash cousins) that makes this island realm seem even smaller than it is. Perhaps because of this, everyone calls each other "aunty" and "uncle," just as the missionaries call one another "sister" and "brother." It is never wise to make a tactless or unseemly comment about anyone, regardless of his color or the cut of his clothes, whether he wears a loincloth or frock coat, because he's likely related to some forty other folks you know , and the remark will get back to him and you'll find yourself revising it while you nurse your wounds after having knuckles for lunch.

This disregard for the subtle distinctions of race presents a noble lesson in tolerance that even the Yankee abolitionists would find instructive. A trip to these islands might just be fatal to prejudice and bigotry!

Such a visit must come soon, or one day, mere decades from this one, rapacious haoles will have ground the pride out of these tawny folk, making them island niggers. But these majestic people may never adopt the slouch of the Negro because they remain on their land no matter who owns it – or thinks he does – not shipped to some distant continent. Accustomed since the ancients first sailed ashore with their little and their simple, the natives can never be reduced by mere poverty to servant mentality. No, it will take business and greed and missionaries to accomplish that!

I have been told often, and always by devoutly Christian folk, that I must not trust a thing one of these Kanakas says. In this kingdom, there is a simple equation for Truth: discount what a man says by 98 percent - the rest is likely to be fact. They <u>*will*</u> *lie and that's all there is to it. But what of it? It's our own fault. We ought not to be asking them things that they have to lie about. If you ask a native will he do something, he's bound to say yes, to be polite, whether he intends ever to do it or not. That's aloha. He doesn't want to make you feel bad, right then. Later maybe he won't be around to witness your disappointment. And don't query a man on the age of the horse he's trying to sell you. It's an invitation to prevarication. It would be so in Yankee territory too, or Washoe. Of a native lady's virtue, make no inquiry whatsoever. Assume it's no better than it ought to be and move on to another subject. In a kingdom that celebrates the prowess of its chief princess's male harem, no one is likely to give you a straight answer about the morals of the women. It matters not a tick. They are a charming, laughing, loving people. That's all a man needs to know. No, don't ask those kinds of questions and you'll find these folks as honest as any others.*

Our friend Lono seems exempt from any of those

traits that others may find villainous in the Hawaiian. He is indeed a fine fellow and seems particularly devoted to Napua. It is for her sake that he makes the trip from town every other day or so with provisions and news. Yesterday he brought word that there was a man on a "good chestnut horse" hunting for me, a haole wearing a felt hat instead of the local style of lauhala or straw, asking questions between here and Kahului. Apparently none of the Kanaka has given us up and revealed our hideout - owing to Napua's influence rather than any feeling for me. The chestnut horse man is not a bounty hunter, I trust, but someone sent by the Union. *I haven't posted a dispatch in weeks and don't intend that I shall.*

It shames me now to think how I wrote in favor of the establishment of the San Francisco - Honolulu steamship line! As if these islands needed mail! Or commerce! Or more haoles to infest the landscape and infect the generous and hospitable Hawaiians! There are enough white faces here already. Capitalists and businessmen - steamers full of them - swarm Oahu and then the rest of the island chain. What value is capital and population in a place where all one's needs are met by the gentle art of barter and the generous hospitality that is Aloha? Revenues are nothing against the ruin that more commerce will bring to these rainbowed islands. Sugar, molasses, rice, salt - the profits all go one way and leave pockets in the United States brimming with customs duties and price shares. Meanwhile I've ridden over miles of fertile land where a scattering of gentle people make their living modestly farming and fishing, husbanding their meager resources, not plundering the land as the haoles do in their sanctified, rapacious way. But mine is an unpopular view of commerce here, sedition that the Union men aren't likely to appreciate. I refuse to write it.

April 29

Moonrise comes later each night as the month hastens on. This is the darkest place in the world when the moon doesn't shine, but on those nights when it does, it bathes all below in its mystic glow. At this latitude, the waning moon hangs like a bowl of milk as it rises, spilling silver onto the sea, tipping as it reaches apogee in the blackest part of the night, then dropping behind the peak of Haleakala, defying everything that I have known about the moon from other latitudes. Napua tells me that Hawaiians measure time by nights rather than days. Each has its own name, olekulua (oh - lay - koo - loo - ah) being this one, and this is the moon month they call Welo, when the aina is abundant after the rainy season.

The stars look to be just beyond my grasp, so close to this little earth as if they had skimmed low across the ocean and bumped into the land unexpectedly. We study the night sky from our makeshift bed. The North Star comes round and then the Southern Cross – Newe

– just beneath the belly of old Centaurus. The ancient navigators used the cross to fix their bearings and plot their course, rigging their canoes like masted rafts to sail the vast Pacific to "green-backed Hawaii" as they most prophetically called the islands. Tonight I seek the fixed North Star as if to get my bearings. In other climes I searched out the Big Dipper, but here I navigate along a different string of stars, the stellar glints of the Polar Star and that old cross, reminding me that I am neither place, not north or south, but landed here in these floating isles, and happy to have found a haven such as hers.

Time is suspended, with eternity in the moment, yet the sickle moon warns that the days are slipping by while I am lost in this divine indolence. Our days are full of nothing, unless you count the pleasure of meandering down to the beach to watch Napua fish or bathing in the mountain-cold pools at the base of the cataract in the river. The languid morning is occupied with our small domestic chores - today it was laundry in the pool. She has shown me how to pound & swish until the crystal water imparts a freshness to my shirt and underthings that no Chinese laundry or Irish housekeeper could give it. But generally I have escaped the captivity of clothes by wearing only a light costume such as any sane person - man or woman - would adopt on torrid days. I've thrown off unseasonable goods, some days wearing only my trousers. I was born modest, but only in spots, and pants cover most of them. I trod barefoot too, with that delectable freedom that boys in summer enjoy.

Of course, women everywhere are accorded a license

in their dress in summer that men are not, enhancing their grace and beauty by the flow and color of their garments. I have always appreciated the delicate fabrics and bright colors of summer garb, the softness and shape that delights both the senses and spirit. Here the ladies have a good deal more freedom and less yardage, native and kama'aina alike. In the island's perpetual summer, one can put on the easy attire of summer in the country, donning the loose, light clothes of that season, apparel that refreshes the body with its ease and coolness. Honolulu streets glisten on a Sunday with white folks suited up in their vanilla vestments with shoes chalked to match. Like New Orleans at Mardi Gras, there is color and gaiety in the dazzling rainment on the streets, a mix of colored skins, and a languor that bedevils the missionaries' intentions. Back East, when the weather grows cold, men and women put off their comfortable dress and don the dismal blacks, the somber browns, the dreary dun of walking coffins that only contribute to the prevailing insanity. Here I am attired in summer every day.

Our afternoons generally pass with a saunter in the neighborhood to some wild glade where guava and papaya and mountain apple and passionfruit offer themselves up for our delight. Napua has the aboriginal faculty in finding food, having learned to gather and fish and forage to produce a meal. She does so without the least hint of pretension, without the fanfare bestowed upon a modern man when he goes off in search of provisions in the wild and returns with his prize. Napua undertakes her provisioning without an attitude of sport or display, simply cultivating, working even the wild land to make our board and bed from the abundance around us. So it is that now I see wild Nature is not benevolent but only benign, not cradling us in her arms but letting us wrest our simple living from her.

Apparently Napua means for me to assist in this work. Thus ends my indolent dream. She undertakes to teach me native fishing, unlike the river angling of my boyhood. Napua muzzles me before we go, insisting we must not speak of fishing – it would alert the fish and sour our luck. I have fished since I could hold a pole but never – in the cold lakes of the Sierras or the muddy Mississippi – have I caught a trout or catfish as delicious as the moi she fishes up. We dine earlier than is fashionable - before dusk - on simple fare, and settle in to watch the night. The nights

Samuel crossed out the start of that last sentence. He would not write of the nights. Napua slipped up behind him now and put her hungry mouth on his bare shoulder. He did not need to write of their nights to remember them. She astonished him with her ease, the way she came to him without shame and offered her gifts to him, bearing his fumbling with grace.

Over the next mountain island - Hawaii - there is an amber glow on the underside of the evening clouds, the reflection of the fire in the crater at Kilauea (kee-low-ay-ah), bright contrast to the silvered night here. She tells me Pele (pay - lay), the goddess of the volcano, is on one of her rampages over there, churning up the innards of the earth. They have a bible's worth of stories about her, her loves and battles, and often it is impossible to distinguish the one from the other. She makes the earth shake and the lava flow in her passions. To hear Napua tell it, she is a woman, like Napua herself, but writ large, and as much a mystery as any woman.

In general, their gods are somewhat more human than ours - and more reliable. We must perpetually placate our God with prayers and oblations, but we can never really be sure of His response. Whether he will show up as that fierce old Father of the Old Testament or the Son Jesus with his gospel of love, it is impossible to be sure which will be in attendance in any crisis. The Hawaiian gods are easily distinguishable by their separate features - one for the rains and one for the volcano, another for the seas - and each having a dominant aspect of beneficence unless provoked to excess. Kanaka always seem to know where they stand in relation to their gods and don't expend a bit of energy on being anxious about it. Last night we were entertaining each other fondly when without warning the island shrugged beneath us. Back in San Francisco, the weekly earthquakes shake a man out of his boots and send timid folk scurrying into the streets and away from rocking buildings. Here under the moon, we were jostled by a shudder in the land beneath us as we lay conversing about sundry deep subjects, and I, being a Christian of that more civilized sort, leapt up expecting hellfire below and tumult above, while Napua, with her amalgam of church doctrine and pagan belief, merely shifted on the mat and laughed - at me, of course. Here in the islands a quake is merely an adjustment in the goddess Pele's attitude, and since I wear no boots to be scared out of, and the shelter around us sways serenely with the motion of its foundation, I settled down and we continued our amusements uninterrupted and with a certain added piquancy. By Napua's account, it was just the island settling into the ocean a bit as it has done often, the lady Pele shrugging her shoulder. That sort of quietude doesn't come with Christianity, and these island folk would probably be better off without the ministrations of the missionaries. In fact, the missionaries would have more fertile fields to till in America. They should leave off converting these good pagans and go home to work at rousing the Christians there who would benefit from a good strong dose of humanity. Leave this land and its people alone. As a policy, wherever one finds a place and people who have not been converted to his corruption, he ought to let them be, because once civilized, they can never be un-civilized.

April ?

I have always avoided early morning, but here I rise much earlier than was my habit heretofore. I find Napua bent over her journal in the dawn, half-peeled and pagan, with her pencil keen and poised - an inspiring sight, I suppose. The missionaries have accomplished, in a mere four decades, a herculean revolution by bringing reading and writing to these natives. A literate citizenry is prerequisite for any humane society, even a monarchy. Here there is none of that fear of literacy that constricts the teaching of the negro, no anxiety of rebellion or retribution. Indeed it seems that the haole fear nothing from the natives but the mai pake and an occasional dose of the venereal. I sometimes detected, back in Honolulu,, a slight anxiety about the lure of Hawaiian ways and the urge to surrender to them -- the seduction of forgetting to don one's coat and cravat and to leave off work at the slightest provocation as natives do to indulge some pleasant whim -- but that is the only risk the haoles seem to recognize, not reading and writing. Yet literacy is the foundation of progress, and it is not revolution but evolution that propels this nation toward greatness.

In general, spreading the English tongue has been a noble enterprise, and yet I have passed all these days without a newspaper or novel, with no ill effect from having only those words that pass between Napua and me, and I find myself content with so much wordlessness. What good does it do a man to tire his eyes squinting at a page of last week's news or some young hack's invention when the only things he needs to know are the beauties and necessities in his dooryard! Even the loss of the borrowed copy of Jarves's prodigious history of the islands that was so useful to me in Honolulu as guide and encyclopedia seems like a gain since I am emancipated to turn my eyes on the world before me and read it instead. I shall have to rely on ocular proof and a newspaperman's powers of observation. Jarves, that true missionary, sophisticated, civilized, well-intentioned, does seem to look through a singularly small set of spectacles, being strong in the details though niggardly in interpretation!

I understand old Adam better and that authority given to him to name creation now that I myself can apply a name to what I see about me. The Hawaiian language with its thirteen letters (most of them k) seems to have few words to indicate distance and relative positioning, as if it matters little where you locate yourself on an island or in paradise. Napua has been tutoring me in the names of things, and though I have not grasped the grammar, I have got a grip on the nouns and can catalogue a good many trees - milo, kukui, kiawe, hala - euphonious appellations, all of them. There is a certain amount of poetry in the names of things in this tongue. Puuwai - for example – (poo-oo-vye) - the heart, but how much more than that is conveyed by that eloquent word: a puu is hill or mound - wai is fresh water, their sacred sap or nectar, and together they express the deepest reverence and understanding of what the heart indeed is.

In proportion as a man knows the language of a place, he understands that place, its people, its history revealed in the cadences and grammar. The Hawaiian language has at least 17 words for adultery - and from this we might come to understand all the subtleties of infidelity and respect so much ingenuity. Regardless of the fine points of illicit love, or "sleeping mischief" as the missionaries called it, the fine levied for adultery in these parts is $30, as a rule, from each of the consenting criminals. The fine for providing strong drink to a native is $500. From these facts we might surmise the distance between the native idea of love's worth and the missionary's.

Napua speaks a perfect American missionary English but lingers over it, setting a languid pace that mimics the soft speech of her childhood. Her own language is perfect and I love to listen to her singing it or trading news with our good Kanaka friend Lono. It is the softest speech imaginable. Every word ends in a vowel, and no two consonants ever collide – there is always a vowel that comes between them. The liquid syllables of her native tongue are flexible, easy, without the hiss of an "s" in it, an ideal language for anything at all you would want to say - until you get mad. Then there's nothing in it to swear with. Not a decent cuss word nor any good insults!

And I am partial to both. I can hardly get through the consternations of a day without them. Only yesterday

I was attempting to shave by feel since I came away without a mirror. The razor, being dull and wayward, took a bite out of my chin and I erupted in a good long string of curses to ease my distress. Napua dropped her work and rushed to my side, clearly frightened by the outburst, and without a trace of sarcasm repeated my oath syllable for syllable. In her voice, without the feeling behind it, it sounded absurdly weak and comically inadequate, ill suited to that lovely mouth and lilting tongue, completely incongruous. And nasty, to tell the truth, being the vile husk of a cuss without its soul. There was nothing to do but laugh, and a good deal of merriment ensued while I explained - or tried to - what a cussword is meant to convey. With a lady's disdain for loose language, she offered me one or two of her native expletives, but there was no bite to them. You can adopt a good many new customs and habits in a new land, but the curses and oaths you were brought up with are the most natural and useful in extremity, which is, after all, the only time you ought to be using them. I know it is wicked to swear as I do – I know it is wrong – I shall certainly go to hell for it, but in certain trying circumstance, urgent circumstances, desperate circumstances, profanity provides relief even prayer can't. Cursing would be the hardest thing to give up, if I stay, though it occurs to me just now that here in the islands there might be few occasions for it. I would try to curb that inclination, for her sake. At least she doesn't try to civilize the cussing out of me.

May ?

In the Sierras it snows at least once a month all year. Here it rains oftener but with that same regularity. A man's hat is necessary to serve as shade and umbrella, often within the same hour. There was more rain today, coming like a mist across the ocean, but when it arrived it was a light drizzle, quite warm and refreshing.

A well-traveled man might think he has heard wind blowing in rain before, but there is no symphony of weather like Hawai'i's – the clatter of palms, the sigh and creak of kiawe, the rush of wind over grass, and the echoing plash of the water just beyond one's sight. This morning after the rain, we sat astride an ancient eucalyptus trunk and watched the coming resurrection. The sun flings banners of iridescence across the sky – purple and gold and such an extravagant splendor as Nature is capable of in the best of places. Every green is silvered with the wetness. There's nothing to compare to the soft colors of Maui on a showery day - it makes her raiment on a sunny day seem almost gaudy. All about us in the canopy, small birds make a gigantic noise. Raising the light, they are flying music.

"Pacific" is a wicked misnomer as far as I can see for this ocean is never pacific and usually looks like fractured glass and froth. Today it is the color of old pewter and heaves as if its surface was oiled. A good day to stay close to the raft, but Napua insisted it was fishing weather. After all, says she, "the fish don't care it's raining." By the time we had precipitated ourselves to the rocky shore, the rain had passed on. Just like New

England weather - if you don't care for it, wait a few minutes.

Anyone who has plied the rivers of America will be astonished at the waters of "Owhyhee." We are familiar with the silt-brown liquid that passes for water in our rivers and lakes and estuaries, while here the ocean and streams that rush to it are clear as crystal so that you can put your hand or foot or whole self in and see the smallest detail as if peering through a fine piece of blue glass. The whole of you is visible along with every mote and mole, each finny inhabitant of the sea that flits past you, every stone and coral cluster.

My companion is a most accomplished fisherman, providing us with choice suppers. Even accustomed as I am now to her disappearing for a while to catch us a batch, I hated to see her go this afternoon, loathing the separation of more than a breath's distance, so I asked to accompany her. It pleased her a good deal, I could see, and she consented. I left off writing, following her through the bush, down the steep declivities, with the earth beneath our feet always damp and a little slippery. We jostled and collided often, making it a very pleasant exercise in spite of the steepness of the slope. The black rock before us glistened and shimmered in the sun - puddles like mirrors giving back the colors of the sky. Napua approached the very edge where the surf beat up against the lava and cast her hook expertly into the foam, jiggling a bit and then hand- over- hand drawing in the first fish of the day and plopping it without ceremony in a crevice where the sea threw up fresh water with every wave, making a handy cache basin.

I do not like work, even when another human is doing it, but watching Napua fish is another thing entirely. With the admiration and pleasure some men take in any expert execution of labor, especially when a comely woman performs it, I delighted in the curve of arm and graceful arch of her back as she dipped bait and waited, like a boy on a jetty. With lithe step her bare feet edged along the lava as she angled for just the right hole that would yield up the bounty. When she had six fish waiting in the rock pool, she bent to the business of cleaning all but one, the first she had caught. She deftly slashed the sandpaper skin behind the head of each, along the belly ridge and spine, gripped the skin and tore it off, revealing the mottled red and white flesh beneath. The blood clung to her fingers, thick and viscous, redder than I had expected against the black rock. It barely mixed with the seawater. With two hands she snapped each head off. This and the innards she tossed far off into the surf before moving to a fresh pool of water to wash her knife, herself and what was left of the fish. A perfect fishwife? I have been with servant girls whose daily labors were no more strenuous or disagreeable than this and found them to be coarsened by their work, but this woman Napua dispenses all that she does with a manner that is fine and full of grace!

As she bent over the work, a slight disturbance on the rock ridge above us loosed a small avalanche that clattered into the trees. That's when we saw him - and he spotted us, I suppose. He disappeared into the trees but not before we saw the felt hat and the chestnut mare Lono had warned us about. Napua thought it best we get out of the open and wait awhile to start back home, but before taking cover, she picked her way along the rocks to a large upright lava pillar placed on its end making a sort of altar. She reverently put the one still whole fish atop the stone - an offering , she said. First fruits. The missionaries have done their best at Christianizing her, but she is and ever will be a <u>*wahine*</u>*. They will never sermonize the pagan out of her. And I would hate to see it. She's generous with her prodigal affections and honest and reverent and resourceful and loving. A slight liberality in her religious practice doesn't matter a bit.*

Spent a pleasant hour (by the sun) in hiding. Didn't smoke, not wanting to give away our concealment. Made no sound at all except for a rustle now and then and a sigh or two.

The scent of old leather and antique paper was comfortable to Emily now as she shifted the journal in her lap. A packet of brittle pages slipped again from within the back cover. Ten sheets of old vellum, torn from another diary perhaps, folded in half and stitched together with something like embroidery floss now gone fragile with age. It was a little book of sorts, a fascicle. Written in a careful hand, with precise and steady roundness the way a schoolgirl learns to write her letters, they were Napua's own diary pages. From within them, a drift of letters fell out. Addressed to "Napua" in care of a Reverend Mr. Finn, they had never been opened. On the back of one, a Sacramento address beneath "SLC" was still clear. Unopened, unread love letters, held all those years. Dead letters unburied. Why? How could her heart not have moved her to tear them open and read them for the love and comfort they might contain? Like other things about Hawaiians that Emily did not yet understand, Napua's pages and the unopened letters would have to wait.

Behind Emily on the bed lay the dress that she had put on and taken off, black, very New York. Now she shifted inside a white dress that she thought scooped daringly at the neck and revealed more of her tender, sun-rosed skin than she was sure she wanted to bare. It was a dress she had bought reluctantly and only at the insistence of Peter VanDyke, her only friend in the university's English department, and it had hung unworn in her closet through last summer. She had packed it at his urging as well. Arching her back and turning her head, she saw how it drifted over her hips behind and swirled around her legs as she moved in front of the mirror. It was a supple lick against her skin. The combination of virgin white and that seductive flare was the dress's appeal, Peter had said.

She met Kamuela at the restaurant, finding him languid and easy in a rattan chair outside on the lanai.

Lahaina was even hotter than usual, and the ceiling fans gave a welcome swirl to the evening air as it settled around them. She was glad she'd picked the place, away from the noise of tourists, as she had hoped. In his lap he held a *lei*, white and fragrant, and not the kind that the tourists bought at airports or supermarkets. "Pikake," he said as he laid it over her shoulders. "My aunty grows it." Emily drew the perfume into herself as he put the wreath of flowers over her head and kissed first one cheek and then the other near the corners of her mouth. The coolness of the blossoms nestled against her skin where the dress bared it.

The host met them just within the dimly lit doorway, assessing Emily quickly as he gathered up two menus. Tall and elegant, with long fingers on his dark hands, he moved gracefully two steps in the direction "this way," before he realized her male companion was not some well-dressed tourist but Kamuela and stopped.

"Aloha, Kam. Good to see you." The two men acknowledged each other with the subtle lift of chin that local guys met one another with. "Wait – let me seat you over here instead." He swerved left, stepping down to a small oceanside dining room away from the hum and music. As he held the wicker peacock chair for her, Emily noted the starched tablecloth and exquisite view from the secluded lanai. Settled into the chair, she realized she was probably all but invisible to anyone but Kamuela.

Kamuela reached out a hand to the host and murmured "Mahalo, Kawika.

"*A ole pilikia*, brah. Enjoy. You like wine?"

"Sure – whatevah you think we like have." It was all transacted so quietly, almost covertly, in their pidgin. Suddenly there was a waiter smiling eagerly at her, alerted to bring her anything, satisfy any request, and thus please Kamuela. Emily assumed he came here often and wondered with whom but knew it was none of her business.

"I met your aunt today. Malia? At the library."

"Yes, she told me. When I went to pick the flowers." He reached across the table with his wide, thick-fingered hands to touch them again.

"You picked these? And made the *lei*?"

"Of course." Her wondering surprised him and embarrassed her.

"Thank you. It is very beautiful. I didn't know men—I mean, I didn't know—I never thought, really, about someone actually making the *lei*." In an instant, she speculated about the gentleness in him, a sort of feminine energy, a bit like the softness in Peter. And Peter was gay. But even across the space of the table between them, she sensed Kamuela's interest in her, an erotic charge that was hot and steady, like sun-heated stones after dark.

He quietly let her think through whatever it was until he saw her come back into focus again, acknowledging him. "Malia." He picked up the thread of conversation and handed it back to her. "My aunty. She says you were very busy and quite insistent."

"I found the information I needed. The journal seems

authentic. It fits the facts. I'm still waiting for materials to come from Honolulu, but I know it's authentic. I'm sure."

"Good. Now you know."

"Who else has seen it – knows about it?"

"Aunty Malia, my cousin Loke, my uncle. The whole *ohana* knows the story though."

"And now will you tell me your part of it?"

"Aunty already told you. It has been in our family since Napua died. She was my great-great-grandmother. Her husband, Lono, gave it to their son, who gave it to my grandmother, who gave it to me. She said I would know what to do with it." He paused to sip the water that had appeared at the table and reflect on how much to tell her now. "The notebook came to Napua - with the letter - after Clemens left Maui to return to Honolulu. He left it behind that last evening, apparently, with Lono. He never knew, probably, that he had left her with something more than that—my great-grandfather." He hesitated and waited for her to react somehow. The wine arrived at the table, and he poured while he spoke. "Sojourners of any worth always leave something behind just as surely as they take something away." Emily bristled at his *kahuna* voice, feeling the distance it created between them. He noticed and shifted toward her easily closing the space across the table.

"He left his name behind. She named him *Samuel,* against Hawaiian tradition."

"What do you mean?"

"Well, until the 1860's, Hawaiian children were

named by the *ohana*, and the name became the child, formed his character, was descriptive of him as he grew. The name might come in a dream or vision to one of the elders or something like that. There were no family names until then when the king created a code to regulate names, and after that, most everyone had a Christian name and a Hawaiian name. He was the only Samuel in the *ohana* until I took the name as mine, but the Hawaiian form, *Kamuela*."

Emily kept focused on the facts. "Was she royal?"

"Not quite the way I think you mean. We are a long line of Hawaiians, but not a royal one. In the time of the great Kamehamehas, ours was an *ali'i* family - the courtly class, with responsibilities, very powerful. They protected the bloodline, trying always to marry higher in the class to gain more *mana*." He seemed vaguely amused rather than annoyed. "All those tales about island princesses are for tourists. Not every haole man who came here bedded a princess. There weren't that many. And haoles weren't very appealing once you got close to them. They didn't bathe often enough. And to the royals, an *ali'i* lineage was important, so they didn't take chances." He seemed to be telling a story that he had had to tell before. He took a long breath and reverently murmured the rest. "Napua was just a Christian-educated Hawaiian girl who rode well and could help out when they needed someone to take Clemens to Hana. It would not have happened if there hadn't been an accident so her brother could not go. Later, when the pregnancy was suspected, the church was scandalized.

Napua had been one of their favorites, from a good family, someone who could help them further their cause as she came into her womanhood. She was a bright star for whom they had very high hopes - as a teacher, certainly, or perhaps a missionary's wife. Their anger would have driven her to despair, but her *ohana* wanted the child. It is our way. *Keiki* - children, babies - they are our best things, even if the child could not be Hawaiian *ali'i.* And later, she and Lono married in the church, and the boy Samuel assumed that Lono was his father. It's all he knew until he was a father himself, and Napua told him the story."

Emily had listened carefully for clues to Aunty Malia's resistance and found none. She had to ask. Kamuela sat back slightly before he answered her question.

"They do not want the publicity. To *haoles*, it is perhaps a great honor to be the child of a famous man, but for the family, the *ohana*, it would bring attention they do not want. They fear it would invite the media and all sorts of people they cannot imagine into our tranquil life here."

"Is there something else?"

"He was *haole*. The Keana'aina *ohana* is proud of being Hawaiian. They have married carefully and kept their Hawaiian blood."

So it was something she could not argue around, at least not yet.

"Then why did you give the journal to me?"

"Always it was said that someday someone would

come for it. And then I dreamed of you, coming like a white bird."

It was such a simple and straightforward answer that Emily, with her talent for subtexts, could hardly credit it. Unconnected completely to money or notoriety, his giving over the journal to her was prompted by something outside her experience of literary ownership, and there was no other motive she could construct. She would have to just believe him for now. He was following voices and traditions she could hardly imagine, but his gaze across the intimate distance of the dinner table was convincing enough. Still, she vaguely distrusted the shaman's wisdom that he exuded when he spoke that way, being unused to men who believed in something beyond themselves.

Their after-dinner stroll down past the old Pioneer Inn and along the seawall was deliberately slowed to take advantage of the softness of the night. The antique brigantine *Cartheginian*, berthed in the marina, added its own notes to the music of riggings on masts all along the waterfront. Against the moonlit water, the old brig stirred Emily's imagination the way 19th century artifacts often did when she was unguarded - they spoke to her of resilience and resolution, of the excitement of being abroad in a young world full of possibilities and ideals, a time less frantic, slower. She realized those were the same qualities she found so appealing in Kamuela. They were becoming friends. The talk between them had been fluid and intimate, not at all the vigorous reconnaissance of dates with other men. She liked him and knew that she would have even without the warm pulse between them. He walked her back to her hotel and waited comfortably at the door while she unlocked it and turned on a light behind the jalousies. She turned to him and let him take her hand again, and when he stepped away, she was sorely disappointed and surprised.

"Good night. Tomorrow, I would like to take you to another beach. A picnic. We have a month, you said. I will show you my island. I'll pick you up. Will seven be too early?"

Emily could only nod. He smiled, kissed her gently near her mouth again and walked out of the ring of light into the balmy night. She watched him go, feeling sad and slighted. The warmth between them had been smooth and safe, and she had wanted to be kissed and then more. The heat where he touched her even incidentally, the smell of him, the teasing line of tattoo that disappeared under his shirt sleeve, the languor in his voice—she had expected he would come inside. She had wanted him to.

Closing the door, Emily felt the cool tiles against her feet for the first time. The disappointment was unfamiliar and tinged with resignation. She didn't think she was very good at sex anyway. It was always a relief to her when whoever it was put on his clothes and discreetly left her to the quiet of her apartment. She appreciated what they gave her, those fragile, learned men - more relief than pleasure - but after the quick spasm, she was seized with anxious energy that propelled her to middle-of-the-night housecleaning or grading student papers and the inevitable feeling that surely there must be more to it than that. More to everything, in fact.

Peter van Dyke's voice over the telephone was crisp and distinct, but the distance created a barely perceptible lag in the transmission that prohibited the usual quick and facile rhythm of their conversations.

"Emily? Is this really you? Where are you? Are you back?"

"I'm still in Hawaii."

"Oh my god --- what's wrong?"

"Nothing." She had to hesitate the space of a heartbeat to let the messages catch up. "In fact, I'm having wonderful luck."

"The Melville story panned out?"

"No."

"You fell in love?"

"Stop it."

"It's bound to happen eventually. I can't keep you forever. You're going to meet someone with a hard-on for you and . . ."

"Stop it!"

"Ok - what's up over in paradise? And it's almost eleven o'clock in the morning here in America, and I have to go teach freshman composition to summer session boneheads, so make my day."

She was surprised at her reticence in telling him. He was, after all, the one colleague she could trust with what might be wonderful news and not worry about a pre-emptive leak or academic claim jumping.

"What's up?!" he said louder, as if the connection was worse than it was.

She told him, in rough outline, about finding the journal, sketched in the facts that supported its authenticity, and then, in the last breath, announced the author: "Clemens. Samuel Langhorne Clemens."

"*The* Clemens? You're sure? Twain? Really?"

"Absolutely."

"The jackpot! Congratulations! When are you coming home? Are you bringing the journal with you?" She was quiet. "Emily? You there?"

"Yes. I'm here. There might be some issue about who has control of the journal. The family may not cooperate and give permission to publish."

"But you have it right now? In your hands?"

"Yes."

"Then copy it. At least do that. Do they have Xerox machines out there in paradise?"

"Of course. Good idea." Even if they would not consent to publication, she could quote from the manuscript.

"So when are you coming home?"

"The end of the month, as planned, I suppose."

"Who is he?"

"Who?"

"The man you're not telling me about."

"What makes you think . . . ?"

"You don't sound as excited as a find like that would make you. Someone is *more* exciting."

"It's not like that, Peter. He's just the man who gave me the journal - Kamuela Keana'aina." She would not tell him the rest of the family history, the genealogy, not yet anyway.

"Hawaiian?"

"Mostly."

"What aren't you telling me?"

"Nothing. Really. We just had dinner. And he took me to the beach once. Nothing."

"You're not having fantasies about going native, are you? Staying for the rest of your life, sleeping on the beach under a palm tree, running around half-naked with your strapping brown lover - he *is* brown, right?"

"That's racist. And beside the point. And no, I'm not having fantasies. I'll be home at the end of my month here, right after the 4th of July, unless I need a little more time to work out rights and all that with the family."

"Em - seriously - I'm excited for you. After this, you can get a job anywhere, and get out of this place - get yourself one of those posh research chairs where you only have to teach a graduate seminar once every ten years. NEH grants, MLA grants, the world will open up for you. Tenure wherever you want it!"

She knew how Peter wished he was someplace else, somewhere less provincial, as he said, not realizing as she did that all English departments were essentially the same. It wasn't about geography but the nature of university life itself. And there were places worse than Buffalo . . . Albany, for instance.

May 2nd - probably

I was born early and until recently I prepared to die prematurely as well. Though it was but months ago, it seems decades since I sat contemplating a pistol or poison as a way out of this world. I am grateful now that I did not succeed in that low moment with the revolver at my temple, but I am not ashamed of it, thinking that it was the portal to this bliss. I believed I had been bankrupt before, but now I see that the deep poverty of my penury was in the awareness of it. Here where pennies are irrelevant, that old pennilessness - and the terrors of it - seem darker still and blessedly distant. Here the worrisome debts and perpetual impoverishment that have haunted me - have pursued my father and all of us - cannot prevail. Instead of wishing I had courage to end my life, I live as though I had done it and now am born again. That other me is dead. The old terrors are dead as well, and I might live here forever without a nagging conscience. I embark now on a second boyhood. Baptized in the waters of Haleakala's slopes, I am risen up anew. And what should this second Lazarus do with his new life?

Leisurely hours mimic the desultory pace of summer

afternoons on the river and bring me to the sweet lassitude of boyhood again, the one I remember, or the one I would like to. Here I might work half the day in pleasant, simple labor - fishing, gathering the fruits of the land, farming, mending what little clothes a man might need - and spend the remains of the day in pursuit of pleasure and repose. Indeed the labor itself is a kind of delight - work and reward being immediately and intimately connected. If I catch a fish, I eat it. If I pluck a mango, it is my supper. If I wash my clothes in the stream, I have not only the freshest wardrobe but the delight of cool waters to frolic in. It costs one so little to live, turning one's back on those expensive necessities that civilized society demands. The specter of poverty that has hovered just over my shoulder has no dominion here. I have spent days skulking about San Francisco with naught but a 10 cent piece in my pocket, low and suicidal with my poverty, but here all a man needs is the price of a cigar – all else is given to him by Nature. It is as if I have stepped through time into a world centuries ago, just a few years from Eden, when simple, vivid living was the rule. Ordinary time has ceased --- and with it, all care is gone, and I happily postpone my death.

Divested of his trousers and underwear so that they might be washed, he was at a loss for something to cover himself with until Napua pulled a length of cloth from her bundle and began to wrap it cunningly around him. When she tied the knot at the waist and tucked the remnants into the final fold, Samuel took a few tentative steps before he began to stride about, savoring the sudden freedom of limb and the movement of air about his loins. With hands on hips he mimicked the sway of hula but managed only to produce a sort of burlesque of it before Napua's indulgence failed her and she frowned. Hula was too sacred for comedy. He did not see that he was an affront to her with his still-pale flesh and knees akimbo and legs like a chicken prancing in the grass or perhaps a drunken sea bird. Bare-chested and still white except for the reddened triangle at his throat where his shirt had opened to the sun, he wore the sarong without the least bit of dignity but a certain pride. Like all newfangled things, the wrap intrigued him. Skirted as he was, he could give up another portion of the swagger and pretense of *haole* men. Already he felt the creep of gentleness and quiet on him, the spirit of Lono that attracted him so, a feminine sort of being. When his clothes were dry, he folded them into one of the storage calabashes and kept the native garb. With neither watch nor wallet, pockets were hardly necessary. In the morning when he woke, he first grabbed the cloth wrap and tied it on, savoring the feel of the air about his nether parts.

May - the 2nd

We are moving today, leaving this little ark to take up residence in a cottage or hale (ha-lay) that Napua knows of nearby, closer to the ocean, the abandoned domicile of some Yankee merchant seaman who jumped ship and planned a life of languor and love here. He died, she says. Of drink. Reminds me that I haven't had a whiskey in - I can't recall. I myself tried a bit of the intoxicating awa (ava) the Kanakas use instead of whiskey. Vile stuff. It numbs the tongue & melts every muscle but leaves the wit behind. I can't think why I would want strong drink here. Inebriate of beauty instead. Flowers that rival the rainbow - languid breezes and blue skies every day - emerald land and azure seas before me. And Napua. My dearest companion of day and night. Woman of sweet ecstasy - Heart's delight - Dear debauchery.

Today we are packing up our meager belongings, putting what we carry into two over-sized gourd bowls - calabashes - and we're ready to be off. Loaded 8 lbs. of goods and 6 lbs. of anticipation. After all the accoutrements of travel that were bestowed on me as I departed San Francisco, (the brandy and extra socks being all that turned up useful), I find that all that's really needed is a change of underwear and a well-made hat. And a few cigars. Napua's little goods seem even smaller since she foregoes the hat and cigars. A change of dress for her is a clean length of cloth to wrap about herself, the shapeless missionary dress having lain in the bottom of the calabash these many days. And there are her fish hooks and a bit of netting, a comb for her hair. My supply of scented soap being used up, we haven't even that to carry. A bundle of fruits and dried fish and yesterday's cooked taro completes our preparations and we are moving.

This evening we see our new home in the soft light of dusk. The bungalow has the allure of a home and some of its comforts, yet I miss the sweet retreat of our little raft that stood so firm above the flood. I've been in many a parlor 3 or 4 times the size of that refuge and felt cramped and smothered by it, but there - with fronds for walls and the breezes rustling through and a solid floor of good Hawaiian wood lashed together against the wet and centipedes—I've never felt more safe and free.

But we had no choice. Yesterday we saw smoke from someone's campfire curling up above the sway of green, the only human thing in all that exuberance before us. We must either move or be found. So we've come to this hermitage. It's a sort of shanty set up on stilts near a stream that doesn't amount to much now but is likely to be a regular Mississippi in the rain. There are two rooms and no door, a verandah—lanai—that droops a good deal at one end but otherwise goes all the way around the outside and provides a sort of umbrella for the place. The bungalow perches in a bit of open space not far from the beach, though trees of all sorts are crowding in on us and moan and whistle and clatter in the perpetual breeze. There's a rude sort of kitchen in one corner and in the other room a Yankee bed of the old style - a wooden frame with a net of hemp to suspend the straw mattress. Having seen a centipede crawl out of the straw, I'll keep to the mats on the floor. The deceased tenant left nothing much behind but silence and a coffeepot, or so I thought until we pulled aside an old sheet of canvas and found a cache of books. The light failed before I could make a fair inventory, but there seems to be a good deal of Shakespeare and Tennyson and a damnable Cooper, a tattered Malory's Morte de Arthur *as well, all read to rags. No Bible. If only we had a cat, it would be domestic perfection. I don't suppose we could find one to rent.*

Fagged out, we still set to work to rid the place of rats and crawling things, dust and mildew. Napua gasped as I, ignorant of any insult, sat down in the doorway to smoke. It was not my vice that disconcerted her but where I practiced it just then. Kanaka hold that one must never sit or stand on the threshold of a house. It is more than unlucky. It is another one of those kapu the dear girl keeps alongside the ten commandments. Napua felt some discomfort on account of the dark hatted horseman in addition to the travesty of the doorway episode, and insisted we must secure our refuge by pissing at the four corners of the place to keep the evil away. Mimi (mee-mee) – that golden fluid is believed to be some powerful sort of deterrent, and I obliged my companion by anointing the foundation of the house copiously. By dark we collapsed into a delicious sleep in our new home.

Remembering how I bemoaned the lack of quality hotels in Honolulu, I confess now that I would rather see travelers to these islands put up in one of these native berths for a fortnight, exposed to the balmy air and soothing quiet, a diet of fresh fish and fruits, and the company of good hearted Kanaka friends. Your California businessman would not take to it - nor his flounced and parasoled lady - but that's no loss, I've come to think. Let them stay in California. I fear that they will spoil this Eden with their economies and travesties of business. I have seen Hawai'i's future in Honolulu and found her past here on Maui, and it is the latter that must be preserved.

Napua is determined to turn the horses loose - says they will find their way back or meander into someone else's yard and he'll know to return them. We could not send them back with Lono because he would be tormented by folks wanting to know where we'd gone to. The owner, being haole, has probably already raised the alarm, thinking them stolen, and may be on his way looking for his property! Natives would wait a good long while before assailing a search, knowing eventually someone would bring the critters home. When it comes to horses, there is a remarkable lack of thievery among the Kanaka.

Kamuela had deliberately kept this adventure for the last of their three days of idleness while Emily waited for the books to arrive at the college library. On Wednesday they had spent the day at a beach on the northern part of the island, beyond the shining resorts of the Kaanapali coast, leaving behind the shoals of tourists and traffic. He had shown her how to fish for *moi*. Thursday they had driven south along the old road to Kihei and beyond, hiking past Makena to a secluded beach at the end of the road. And at the end of that day, he had left her at her door with a kiss so deep and tender that she trembled when he moved apart from her and walked out the door with the promise that he would pick her up at 4:00 the next morning. He did not tell her where he was taking her, but after those easy days of walking, talking, sharing food and sunsets and sea, it did not matter. She would go anywhere he would take her, she knew. Somewhere along the way, the hunger in her had become a hum, the edge of need softened to something else, and Emily was left quietly alive in her body for the first time she could remember. She felt the breeze ruffle the hairs along her neck, the play of sun and shadow on her skin, the sound of the pulse in her ears as she rested on the sand beside him after a swim, and then in the night the cool rasp of sheets across her back and thighs where the sun had given her a kiss of color.

She rose at 3:30, showered again, and lavished her skin with the lotion he had given her. The kukui oil in the concoction made her honeyed arms and legs glisten slightly. Her hair seemed too short to her now, but she secured it with a flower as he had taught her to do. She was ready when he tapped on the door and whispered her name, not wanting to wake any of the other guests.

His face lit with a mischievous smile when she stepped to meet him in the doorway.

"Pants." He looked her up and down, appreciating her at the same time. "I forgot to tell you - pants. It will be cold up there." Only then did Emily notice that he was wearing jeans and a denim jacket and hiking boots instead of his usual thong slippers and shorts. She stepped into the bedroom and slipped into her khakis and sneakers, and when she turned around, Kamuela stood against the light in the doorway. The bed lay between them. In the dimness, he quickly took in the intimate disarray of woman-things. It was four steps across the carpet to each other and a kiss so deep that she began to feel that he was already inside her. Fitting front to front, gripping each other, they kissed a long time until she felt the swelling against her straining, and Kamuela pulled away insisting that they must hurry or "miss it." She drew in a long breath and followed him, a little angry, a bit of a bruise on her lip.

Leaving his old blue Toyota in the numbered space reserved for hers, he drove her car as if it was familiar. The night closed around them while they cruised the nearly empty road down the west side and then across the island, then a hard right and a climb, not toward Hana this time but upward to the summit of Haleakala volcano. Along the way, he told her the story of the demigod Maui, how he had harnessed the rays of the sun from the mountaintop and negotiated with the gods for longer days of sunlight so that his mother's tapa cloth could dry. Haleakala - "house of the sun" - where there truly were more hours of daylight than on the land below. They were headed for the sunrise.

Below them, lights danced in flirtatious patterns, and above them the stars mapped heaven, and far off where there could be only the dark waters, a fishing boat flashed an occasional beacon. The road narrowed and switched back on itself, edging the steep sides of the old volcano, zigzagging upward. The rumble as they crossed an old cattle guard anticipated the specter of a cow looming at the roadside where she was keeping warm against the night. An hour later, they were at the summit. Emily stepped from the cocoon of the car into the cold wind. The thin layer of ice and frost over the volcano's cinder mantle disappeared wherever she stepped. Kamuela wrapped her in a blue blanket and led her toward the east-facing edge of the dark crater. Already the sky at the horizon was lightening to a dazzling purple, and the stars began to fade into the morning. Far out over the sea, the undersides of clouds began to silver and streak the dark sky. Then the rose and lavender and vermilion began to build until half the dome of heaven was a garden of brilliant tints, a sunset in reverse, the colors of creation. She did not have words for what she felt but retrieved a favorite bit of poetry. "Fire and ice," she whispered as much to herself as to him. "*Some say the world will end in fire/some say in ice . . .*"

"*From what I've tasted of desire*," he picked up the poem where she had paused, *"I hold with those who favor fire*."

"*But ice is nice and will suffice*," she finished.

Neither was surprised that they both held the poem in their mouths and memories.

Emily opened the blanket and invited Kamuela in. They leaned into the light as it climbed and kissed the rock and rubble around them, lighting the world that they could see. Night gave way. Day came again. Light saved them. The air they breathed was just barely warmer. "Clemens said it was the 'sublimist' spectacle he'd ever witnessed," Kamuela murmured to her. "The ancient ones thought so too, the priests of the old time. This place and this moment were sacred to our *kahuna*."

Emily looked about her in the brightening light. There were a few families swaddled in hotel blankets, tourists in couples, some perhaps honeymooning, a New Age group softly chanting, a shivering Buddhist monk in saffron and maroon staring not at the sky but at the rocks. Kamuela led her over slipping cinders up to a higher place and pointed south to where Mauna Kea and Mauna Loa loomed above a lei of clouds over on the Big Island. The sunrise had given them back the world. Huddled against the chill wind and darkness behind them, Emily understood the primal terror of night, the relief that the sun had come again, an affirmation of the world's order. When she looked at Kamuela, he saw it in her face and knew he had risked rightly.

The trip down the mountain was slower for them

both. The land tumbled and leaped in steep volcanic crags, offering unfolding views of fields and coastline waking to the day. Lunatic tourists on bikes careened past them in small herds and were waiting at the breakfast cafe at the bottom of the mountain. Kamuela kept driving.

His place. He pulled in without saying it, but she knew immediately where they were having breakfast. The bungalow was not even visible from the road, nestled as it was in a grove of kiawe and palm. The unpainted cedar board and batten and rusted metal roof suggested otherwise, but everything else about the little house on stilts spoke of immaculate care. The door was newly painted the color of the ocean in the morning. She stepped up onto the lanai that ran around the house like a hat brim and over the darkly polished threshold, tugged her feet out of her sneakers and eased onto the cool *lauhala* mats that carpeted all three rooms. Kamuela threw open the windows on every side. Morning streamed greenly in bringing birdsong and the creak of trees.

The kitchen that ran along two walls of the central room still bore the trace of his having coffee before dawn, but other than the half-full pot and an empty cup at the side of the sink, the whole place was meticulously cleaned and arranged.

Married, she thought. Damn. She had checked his left hand that very first day at the church, automatically, the way single women do. No ring. He was so free with his time, and that flower he had worn over his right ear - the "single and available" side. She was still speculating when he turned to ask her about breakfast. Kamuela slipped his hand beneath the cropped hair on the back of her neck and drew her to himself.

"Hungry?" he murmured against her mouth. She could not answer him except to close her eyes and wait. He pulled away and turned to the cupboards. "Ok - I'll cook."

Emily lost her certainty and her balance and gripped the edge of the counter, leaning into it, all hope and no more expectation. He was making coffee, pressing open the soft rippling edges of the filter with fingers she could not stop watching.

"The volcano - Haleakala - it has been quiet for a long time," he said so softly that she had to lean toward him.

"How long?"

"200 years. *Kahuna* say there is much heat and fire there, only waiting."

"Dormant."

"Yes, but underneath, the goddess Pele's passions."

"Do you think she will erupt again?"

"I hope so." He looked at her as he opened the coffee can and dipped into it. He measured the coffee and listened for the first percolating gurgle before he said anything more. "When it is time, when the forces of her being rise and gorge her thighs with hunger, when she feels the pulse in her, when she cannot contain her impulse to create, then she will pour her love out."

"Is it dangerous - right here?"

"There is always some risk in passion."

"Will there be a warning?"

"The ones who know her will know when." His hands slid along her curves, pressing softly against the places where she held herself away from him. Emily's cool desert temperament began its surrender, warmed and moistened by his touch, like morning rain on her. Between her legs was nectar.

"Have you ever seen her erupt?"

"Yes, at Kilauea, over on Hawai'i Island." He was whispering now, drawing her closer, arching to fit against her, letting her feel his hardness. "It is as if she wakens. From the core, the heat of her body insists on its wisdom. Her heart pumps hot blood, up, up from her deepest parts" - with one hand he touched the place her heart should be - "over the crust of other wakenings, other loves, memories, as if it was the first time again" - his fingers held her breast reverently - "the land is veined with her heat - she licks, steams, melts" - he bent his head to her neck and swept his lips along the smoothness, taking in the summer smell of her - "she touches the sky with her tongue" - his mouth opened hers to dark, wet probing. Like breath between kisses he whispered "She is wanton, wind, currents, fever, moaning, shuddering." Lips beyond speech held and sought and held again. Wild hands unraveled each other's clothes, dropped the pieces careless as crumbs across the room to mark their path to the bed.

Emily knew exactly what she needed to get to her pleasure as quickly as possible, before she was left disappointed, and she began to move urgently against him.

"Wait," he murmured and stopped her with his hands. "Let me." Surrender was not her habit, but Kamuela was insistent in his stroking, hypnotic as waves. The quiet urging of his eloquent fingers pulled her beyond her own insisting, and she let go of herself. His mouth and hands and all his parts roused her to pleasures that seemed enough in themselves until her center broke open to him and she came wild beyond knowing anything. She could not even be sure he was finished but knew that he kissed her eyes softly and lay finally breathing deeply beside her.

They slept. The second time, she took care of the condom, savoring his body, touching his curves, tracing the long tattoo down the curve of his arm and finally holding him, hard, excited, and she was a little afraid of the power of him and where he had taken her before. All she had really wanted or expected was the sweet release of a shared bed, no entanglements but sheets. Now here was Kamuela, seeming to want more, knowing there was a deeper hunger and how to rouse it. He wanted her passion as much as his own, and something left over when they were spent. Something to last. Nothing less than transcendence.

The day's heat shimmered around them in the low room. Emily wrapped herself in the cloth he had left hanging on the bedpost for her and went to find the bathroom, going soundlessly across the smooth-matted floor. The little house was filled with green scents - the freshness of *lauhala* matting beneath her feet, the whispering kiawe outside the screenless windows, an herbal nuance she could not name. Everywhere she looked there was something growing or a simple clutch of flowers or a drift of soft fabric artfully draped, even over the squared hulk of what must be his computer in the corner. Even the wall of books smelled faintly organic. In the bathroom, as every other place she could see, there was no obvious trace of a woman. The undraped window was filled with narrow shelves each holding a row of old glass fishing floats that bowed the light from outside, a curtain of blue-green glass, bringing in the colors of the sea, shadows that reminded her of his eyes as they had lain skin to skin. The flash of her image in the long mirror on the back of the bathroom door startled her. She did not recognize at first that it was she herself. The bright blue sarong with its bird of paradise design folded itself lovingly along her slopes, languidly knotted across her breasts just where her flesh was getting golden. She saw beauty and was surprised.

"You were a long time coming," he spoke softly as she stepped across the small room. She misunderstood him at first, thinking he meant to critique her as at least one other partner had. "But now you are here. You could stay."

She only looked at him naked and soft in the tumble of sheets, startled at his suggestion and drawn back to the bed.

"There is an opening for an English instructor." She knew what that meant - the remedial classes, bonehead English, too many courses each term, endless dull, error-riddled papers, no time or money for research or writing.

"I'm going back to New York. In three weeks. Twenty-two days." To think otherwise was crazy. People - people like her - didn't fall in love and leave everything behind for . . . for anything.

"Come back."

She moved back to the edge of the bed and tugged at the quilt.

"I mean come back from New York. Come back to me. *Hoi, hoi hou.*"

She was not hungry for the pleasure that time, not at first anyway, but kissed him and then slid into sleepy desire rather than answer him. They went slowly, languidly, softly into each other without caring how it might end or if it would or where it would take them. There were only their textures and sighs and gentle urgings and finally sleep.

It was afternoon when she woke. Light glided across the floor and lit the bed. She smelled food and rolled over to look across the little house into his kitchen. Before she could rise, he came to her with a tray brimming with what he hoped she would like - eggs, bacon, pungent sausages, biscuits, a hamburger, fried rice, and mugs of thick coffee. He tossed back the covers, arranged the wrap he had tied around his waist, and sat cross-legged beside her. He fed her. When they were finished, she watched the shadows on his bare back as he washed the dishes. In the quiet, she considered the books that filled the shelves along the opposite wall, many with titles she didn't know, some in what she thought must be Hawaiian, and in one corner a whole line of Mark Twain titles that ended with the crisp blue cover of the latest biography of him. Emily was impressed. Above it, a collection of Frost's poems caught her eye.

He interrupted her just as she reached to take down the book of poetry. "Shower?" he asked. She nodded. He stepped into the bathroom and returned with towels, leading her out a back door she had not noticed, into the heat and dimness of the trees. Barefoot and half naked, they stepped on smooth river stones embedded in the red earth, a curving path to an ingeniously secluded shower behind the house. Hibiscus and *ti* plants in aquamarine pots hid the mechanics and themselves as they bathed, soaping each other with the familiarity of spent lovers. Emily started out of her ease when a branch cracked nearby. "It's nothing - the land is mine right down to the high water line at the beach - rather, it is my *ohana's* land - and no one comes in here. No one will see."

The copies of the books and articles she had requested at the library arrived in "Hawaiian time" on the fourth day. She was almost disappointed. That meant she had to get to the research. She fell quickly to work, holing up in her hotel room most of each day, but then Kamuela's invitation to the seductions he offered amounted to insistence, and Emily felt too much to maintain the distance and hard focus she was used to. Nights and early mornings were theirs, but after breakfast they parted - sated, reluctant, languid from a half night's sleep. And so the two weeks went, and each day it was harder to surface from their slumber and click into gear for what she thought had to be done. They did not talk about her work or his, and there were long stretches of eloquent silence. Sometimes they spoke of Maui, its parts, the beauty, how things were and why. Kamuela was simply present to her, so she never needed to ask about anything. She would admire a view or a flower and he would tell her the story, how it got its name, who brought it to this farthest out place, what medicines it was used for. Encyclopedic and poetic, he gave her Hawaii piece by piece as she was ready for it.

Meanwhile she was amassing a heap of tentative conclusions about Clemens' state of mind during his Maui weeks and a list of ideas for articles. The niggling doubt about authenticity was finally allayed completely when the facsimile pages from his other journals arrived. The scribbles and markings, the punctuations and abbreviations, even the penmanship, matched what she held in her hands. It had been easy to track down the "Burlingame" referred to - Anson Burlingame, the US Minister to China – and "Jarves," the author of a book lent to Clemens for a resource, a book lost and never returned, apparently. Jarves, a newspaperman like Clemens, had written a useful history of old Hawai'i that Clemens had used a good deal for his background information. The other journals of his were scribbled reminders, snippets of conversation, words and phrases, a jumble of ideas encoded. The one Kamuela had given her was more languid, a connected exploration of his thoughts. There was enough in the journal for several essays and maybe a book. The shift in his authorial voice, the new biographical information that was sure to connect to later works, his developing race consciousness, his relationships with women, maybe even the source for some of Huck's story - all fodder for the academic industry. And all of it could be told without disclosing that a child had been born, and perhaps even Kamuela's connection. Each day Emily converted the raw bliss of Clemens' love affair into the refined and sterile generalizations that the business of professoring required. The question of permission to publish remained submerged. They didn't discuss it, and Emily didn't think about it, but as she sketched out the skeleton of her next few years' work, her hand tired, cramped, and finally refused to hold a pen.

May 5

Today we were explorers, and Napua improvised a route that runs higher up the shoulder of Haleakala to visit one of the waterfalls there. We met no one on the trail. "Trail" is an overstatement. There were no huts or <u>*hale*</u> *along the way, permitting good progress in our journey that otherwise would have been interrupted at every dooryard for a visit to "talk story" as she says. Up there we ambled through copse and forest brimming with birds and flowers I had not yet made acquaintance with, and to one and all Napua introduced me with the delight of a housewife strolling through her own back-door garden. Napua and her kind speak the language of the birds and rocks and trees, the words that white men never heard or have forgotten. The natives intimately know each creature and plant and pass along a road or path with a nod and a good-day! to the inhabitants of wood and wild. Where one's destination is paradise, there is ample time to loiter and gaze and palaver and what you will.*

In America, it seems a traveler hurries from hamlet to city or the reverse without ever seeing the route at all, only pressing forward to his destination, casting perhaps a cursory glance at a prominent rock or hill, especially if it bears some other man's name, barely hesitating as he concentrates on getting the journey done and being safe again in a place that has been baptized as well. "Where are we?" he might ask his companion and be satisfied only with the distance in miles or minutes to the next town, neither curious nor content with the place around him because it is unnamed. Indeed, for any place to be a place seems to require naming. The impulse in Americans to claim the unmarked, unmapped vastness is somewhat diminished in their frantic rush from place to place in the West, but in America, places are their names, and it is fashionable to be derivative instead of descriptive, so there is a burg named after

Pitt, for example. In Hawaii, the democracy of creation ensures that every byway, creek, cave, blossom and tree is known by its own lovely appellation.

Whether it is latitude or attitude, being surrounded by water both insulates and isolates a man. I begin to forget that there is a rest of the world. All I see each day is the edge of my universe, its beginning and end. All else is wave except this peaceful planet. Nothing here is newsworthy by my old standards. What startling bulletin could I make of the sun's rising above crystal seas as it always does - or a drumming rain at night that leaves the air scented with jasmine and eucalyptus - or the perfect poetry of palms undulating in a restless trade wind? The rest is pointless fret and bother got up to sell papers and agitate a man to keep him moving and making money. White men are impatient, suspicious, fidgety, feverish, restless, terrified of boredom and a lack of business. The steady habits of old New England have degenerated into a modern frenzy that drives a man to the brink of suicide. Hawaiians balk at the haole way of work, preferring – quite sensibly – to rest or surf during the hottest part of the day and go to work early and late. They are not keen on how the haoles pay, either. Kanaka are unused to waiting for the fruits of their labors – if they fish, they eat, or dig taro, they eat. Working for the plantation until Saturday payday chains a man to the job. Here a man can work 4 hours to supply all he needs and have the other 20 for pleasure. The result is a rapturous tranquility that renews a man for the next day's enterprise.

Back there a man's time is spent in business, a woman's in pastimes. Here a man and woman might work together side by side, sharing the slight weight of their labors and lengthening the hours of pleasant intercourse. One might wish they could export this ease and comfort to those bustling, greedy, lean cities of America as readily as they do sugar! There's an obscene rumor that Claus Spreckles, a sugar man from California, is figuring a way to run a mill over on Oahu for 24 hours a day - rigging up lights - an abomination bringing that sort of Yankee ingenuity to these islands! He ought to be sent home or hung.

May 6

Hawaii lies before me waiting, a book I will never read all the way through - nor do I want to, because to do so would take away the grace, the beauty, the poetry of it, just as piloting ripped the romance from that book of my youth, the Mississippi. The scenery here surpasses anything I have ever seen. It is sublime. Simply that. A hack might throw a whole dictionary worth of words at the page for description, but it is useless attempting to convey the power of it by giving its dimensions, measurements, colors, varieties of plant life. If I were to tell how many feet high a waterfall loomed and how many gallons of water flowed over it, would anyone know its awesome beauty better? The reporter in me has given it up - I don't want to plumb the inner workings of the sugar trade or dissect the subtleties of the royal court.

I want only this peace. The reportorial instinct in me is dormant or dead, and the $20 per dispatch that the Union *is paying me seems too cheap a price for giving up this elemental life and telling their old lies.*

Haoles look back and forward too much, missing the only time we can be absolutely sure of – the present. This moment is a fact that our Kanaka friends grasp, and they live accordingly, not in memory or anticipation but in this divine now. My days pass without my once mourning the timepiece I have lost. Here time requires no watch at all, though since the missionaries came with their talk of eternities, some native folks in town begin to harken to the hourly chime instead of simply following the rhythm of the day.

I will stay here, where no mail or streetcars intrude, where a man might spend his days among good-hearted natives in wrap-around clothes or none at all, eating poi and fish and fruits, and being thankful to all their gods for such simple fare, giving up housekeeping and debt to simply live reveling in innocent indecencies, surrounded by the scent of jasmine and damp, the mountain clad in all her greens, the tranquil dawns, and Napua. I would be an old man here and never go back to America. And after I have lived on Maui, Heaven could never suffice. St. Peter will be surprised to get a "regrets" from me before he has even sent the invitation, but I choose Hawai'i for my eternal home. What could the charms of heaven be compared to these? What choirs as sweet as birdsong? What ethereal spirit as refreshing to the soul as scented rain? What angel as sacred to me as Napua? In paradise with her, I will rest in peace. Imagine Eternity here, days and nights without end, Napua beside me, our children gathered in the dusk around us.

It was the thought of children that stopped him. Children of a color he could not imagine - like Napua? cinnamon skinned? with hair as black as hers? Or ehu? It was a consequence he had considered before but dimly, having nothing but backroom men's talk to rely on for information and trusting that Napua knew some native secret to prevent such a thing.

Brown skin is always beautiful, while beauty in a white complexion is rare. Native skin, the color of spice, never looks naked, and makes the white face seem somehow unwholesome, ghastly, garish even, needing cover and concealment. The restful, pleasant nutmeg tint of natives is rich and warm, harmonizing with the rainbow palette of nature and humankind, though setting off the haole to disadvantage in a crowd. It is remarkable how their beauty, when mingled with white mongrel blood, brings out the best of pale features. It is a tragedy of our time that mixing races requires percentages and certifications when all a nation truly needs to declare for each of its people is "citizen."

May 8 - or thereabouts –

The Pleiades appear low in the sky at dawn now. No

need for calendar or almanac here – one reads the stars instead.

Last night I woke to wind whispering in the forest canopy. I had been sleepwalking again. Beside me in perfect quiet stood Napua. Rising from our sleeping place, I had stepped onto the lanai and into moonlight. Napua says it is just my body chasing my spirit as it wanders across the cosmos. Having slipped out of my body through the tiny hole at the corner of my eyes, it has run off to see the world, and I am trying to catch up. The dreams that propel my night time perambulations are idle visions, says she. She promises a native concoction of 'awa will cure me of my somnambulism. That vital herb is good for whatever ails you, it seems, even women's worries.

How can it be the moon is once again so near full? A month gone and I've done nothing but cling to this serenity the way a man caught in a current clings to his boat. The moon worked its witchery as Napua stood beside me in the glint, and though I felt her fingers twined in mine, it was near impossible to see the difference in our skins, the lines of color obscured by the night. The warmth of her beside me in the cool, ginger-scented air, the press of her shoulder against my chest, the weight of our sweet delirium - I love her, damn me, I do. I'll stay, stay and be husband to her, and not care a bit for the consequences. If loving her is evil, I'll choose wickedness and go to hell. Here - with her - there's only the sea for boundary and no allure beyond the pleasures of this place. Far from hurly burly streets and airless parlors, on this speck of land in this huge ocean, despite the insistent fact of the land's end always in view, a man feels free, unlimited, unbounded. Back there, I was always wanting to know what was on the other side of the rise, lurking beyond the horizon. Even with all its vast lands, the old continent felt small and confining compared to this. I'll stay. There the harshest daylight would always be upon us, the glare of society's scrutiny - and contempt. It would kill her and maim me. Better to live here in moonlight and golden sun, free and easy and safe from the white man's disdain for difference.

I'll stay. I am lost and wish to remain so! Perhaps now that I've been gone so long, they'll think I'm dead and leave off searching.

The phone rang so many times that Emily almost hung up. Finally, Peter answered.

"Em? It's absolutely karmic that you should call right now, this minute when we were talking about you! Aloha or whatever!"

"We?"

"Um - yes. *We.* A late breakfast after a long and wonderful night. But that's a story for when you get back. Wait! Are you back? Oh shit! Was I supposed to pick you up at the airport today?"

"Peter - what is the matter with you?"

"Nothing. Everything is sublime, in fact. Life is

beautiful. I just lost track of what day it was."

"Who's there?"

"You don't know him yet, and that's why we were talking about you. I want you to like each other. It's important."

"Oh, Peter! You fell in love! It's about time!"

His voice dropped. "Girlfriend - it's *always* been about time." They let it sink, that jaded old argument they so often had about living and loving in the age of plague.

"You sound happy, Peter, and I am so glad."

"Thanks, Em. And what about you? Today's . . . um, the first of July. You're not due back for five days. New developments?"

"I'm staying awhile longer. I just rebooked my flights - I'll be back in four weeks - the first of August. I'll e-mail you the rest, but I didn't want you to rearrange your fourth of July weekend around me needlessly."

"Still having trouble with the Twain family?"

"Not really. And they aren't the Twain family - their name is Keana'aina. There are just some things I need to work out here."

"It's *him*, isn't it?"

"Ok. Yes. It's Kamuela. That's Samuel in Hawaiian."

"Samuel. As in 'Langhorne Clemens'?"

"His great-great-grandson. That's who gave me the journal."

"And a great deal besides, apparently."

"All I know is, I'm going to spend some more time here right now."

Peter sighed the way he always had when he was thinking about Ben. "Em, ever since Ben died, ever since I decided to live in spite of it, I've been looking over my shoulder expecting to get sick myself or lose someone else or - worse - fall in love again. And so we've been doing our pathetic little dance, you and I, working and living in our heads and shoving down the loneliness, trying to stay in the same old place because doing anything else is too risky. We might find joy, and that would be too painful. It's time to give it up. Give yourself the present, Em. You've spent a decade living in the nineteenth century. Choose now, for a change." The phone line hummed with silence. "Stay. The rest is pointless fret and bother."

"Who said that?"

"I did."

"I mean—I thought it sounded familiar, as if you were quoting someone. Peter, are you as happy as you sounded when you answered the phone?"

"Happier. And scared. It was easier being Ben's widow. I know how to love someone to death. Loving someone *alive* is going to be a challenge. But it's time. And you - you haven't loved anyone but me since - I don't know when - since before you finished the last of those rancid romances you were always running away from. If this feels good to you, stay with it."

"Thank you. I didn't need your permission, but thank you."

"Em, I love you. So I have to ask, as best friend and advisor, what's up with the notebook?"

"I've been working with it. I've copied it. I still have it."

"It doesn't sound like it's as important anymore."

"Or maybe important in some way that I don't know yet."

"You talk like Yoda."

"I've been getting *kahuna* lessons."

"What?"

"Shaman. Never mind. I'll be moving out of the hotel, but I don't know where to yet. If you need to talk, call me at his place," and she gave him the number. "Stay happy, Peter. Aloha."

It had been much easier to rearrange her life and travel plans than Emily had anticipated. Fortunately she had not yet turned into one of those slightly eccentric professional bachelors with a cat and jungle of plants, so there was nothing back there to take care of. While that eased her, it also made her unexpectedly sad. Maybe, she thought, there were supposed to be more reasons to be in a particular place than she had to be in Buffalo. When she called her parents, they were only mildly surprised and perhaps pleased, having grown used to their daughter's unrelenting hard work and sacrifice for her profession. Besides, they were in Texas where her father had retired into a cluster of old military men and their wives. She hardly ever saw them. On her way to Kamuela's house, she picked up the newspaper and prepared to look for a cheap rental, a studio probably, somewhere away from the scuttling tourists.

She was waiting for him when he came home from the church but didn't rise to embrace him when he came through the open door. "What's this?" He was amused. "The paper is more important than me? I guess the romance is over." His feigned petulance revealed a slight anxiety. He was only too aware that the number of their days together was ebbing.

Emily peered over her reading glasses in a way that she hoped looked inviting and patted the place next to her on the *punene*. Kamuela, settling snug against her, looked at the classified, "Vacation Rentals."

"What are those red marks for?"

"Studio apartments. The blue ones are rooms. I don't think a room is big enough, but anything larger costs a bit more than I can pay, I think."

It was a short discussion, and he made it easy for her. While the dinner dishes waited in the sink, they drove into town and back, moving her small bundles of gear and her one-suitcase wardrobe into Kamuela's house.

May 9

He very nearly discovered me today, and would have

too, except for Napua's quick thinking. We never heard him coming down the slope - must have had slippers on that chestnut horse. We were lounging after our midday meal, as usual, in the shade at the end of the lanai where the roof dips drunkenly down. Lucky for me she's got the instincts of a hunter and alerted me just as his felt hat appeared through the greenery. I made a hasty retreat into our little house while she concocted a distraction for him. He asked a few questions that I could not distinctly hear, and then rode off in a great hurry as if the devil was after him.

Samuel lurched through the door into the dark rooms and hid himself near the window so that he could hear. There was the creak of saddle leather as the man shifted himself to address the waiting woman. Napua sidled out of the shade so he could see her well. He slipped into smooth courtesy at the full sight of her.

"Good day, miss." Samuel imagined the touch of the man's hand to his hat brim. "I am looking for a man," he insisted without preamble, just like other *haoles* who went straight to business with no talking story or making acquaintance as native people did. Napua did not reply except to smile widely at him as if to confirm that *she* was certainly not a man.

"A *haole* man - red-haired - with a mustache. I don't suppose you might have seen him?" His eyes quickly took in the shanty and their domestic details, surveying the ripening fruit arrayed on the railing and the water gourd suspended by the door. Napua stepped toward him and shrugged until the top edge of her sarong slipped a bit to reveal an inch of roundness.

"Is there anyone else here? Is there a man here with you?"

The menace in the question made her bolder. This kind of waterfront *haole* was easy to manage, especially if he'd had a bit of whiskey and some sun, but this one was hunting and not as easily distracted. He dismounted and stepped nearer while his gaze shifted quickly to the beauty in front of him and then back to the house.

"You alone out here?"

"My father is within the *hale*."

"Father? " He looked around her, squinting into the doorway dimness.

"He sleeps now. He is not well."

"Perhaps I could just have a word with him." He dropped the reins and stepped nearer to her. The felt hat shaded his face, but Napua could see his hungry look.

He had heard the warning in her voice, but at the same time his eye caught the curl of smoke from the pipe Samuel had left behind on the railing in his retreat. Napua saw him notice it, reached for the pipe and held it as she had seen Samuel do. To complete the effect, she put it to her lips and drew a bit of smoke off it, holding it in her mouth a moment before blowing it directly into his hovering face.

He did not flinch. "What kind of sickness did you say?"

"The worst kind. That is why we are here. You won't tell anyone you found us, please. It is very bad with him. He will not live much longer. Then I will burn the house and go."

"The worst kind? You mean . . .?"

"*Ai*. He is a leper."

The hunter rubbed his fingers on his dusty trousers as if he had touched filth. He looked hungrily at Napua but mounted his horse instead and scurried upslope into the trees as if a devil chased him.

Samuel came out of hiding to find his companion with his pipe dangling in her hand and tears spilling over her lashes. "It was a bold stroke! What is it? Did the smoke make you sick, dear?"

"I lied to him. A lie is a sin, Maka. And I said a terrible untruth about my father, inviting the gods to give him the *pake* sickness." She spat the words at him. These were points of morality and faith that he would not debate with her, seeing how much it had cost her to breach them for him.

Napua has gone off alone bearing offerings to make amends to her personal gods, her aumakua (ow-ma-koo-uh) the spirit ancestors who watch over her and her ohana particularly. Two days ago we heard an owl nearby. She waited most of the morning until it swooped just inches from her shoulder. She says it is pueo (poo-ay-oh), the transformed spirit of a foremother. Says it protects her in the forest, brings messages, advice, warnings. Maybe so. Out here beyond the reins of her Christian companions, she reverts to ancient ways more and oftener. She wears her Christianity like the calico over her paganism, doffing it when there is necessity and leaving it off when there is any immediate danger such as today's alarm.

I cannot help but worship a woman so utterly free of guile. It was, I suppose, her first lie. Having been raised a Christian, I know the delight of forbidden fruits and enjoy a good bit of prevarication now and again. I can lie like a senator, to tell the truth. But for Napua there was no delight even in the novelty of it. Only the sorrow of transgression and fear that the lie she had spoken would become an awful truth. Such is the power of the word for her. That she has lied for me seems to put a certain responsibility on me, a yoke not altogether uncomfortable or unwelcome, though I wear it as an indictment of my own proclivity for exaggeration, prevarication, and embroidering the truth. For Napua - and Lono too - words are precious by virtue of their veracity and the power they contain to make things come to pass. A word unleashed has the power of ancient creation behind it, sorcerer's strength, the curses of Merlin, beyond any calling back or cancellation. This accounts, no doubt, for the brevity and precision of their conversations. The word once spoken becomes what is, and so they are fastidious in what they say. The gentle quietude we haoles have ascribed to them springs from this belief. It shames me now when I reflect on all the fibs I've fabricated in my time. My morals in that quarter are entirely lapsed, though I have been tempted much less of late owing to my audience. I would rather have her good opinion of my moral nature than any fifty clergymen. The "gospel according to Napua" is a good deal more Christian in its heathenism than theirs in its theology. I fear I shall never be as upright as she is in her way, and a man cannot be entirely comfortable without his own approval.

When Emily came up from the beach, the warmth of the path seeped into her whole body through her soles. Kamuela had laid down river stones, hard-washed to smoothness by the surges and currents where a river flowed into the ocean, pounding, dragging, tossing the stones against each other until their jagged edges wore away and they were softly rounded. He had told her this as if it was important, a lesson about himself and life, and then he had waited, like a teacher watching to see if his pupil has taken it in.

As she stepped through the doorway, he was listening intently to a voice on the answering machine that Emily recognized immediately. "There's one for you," Kamuela's voice smiled. It pleased him that even these parts of her life were beginning to merge with his. It was the same kind of pleasure he felt when she had put away her laptop and started taking her e-mail on his computer. Now she pushed her hair back over her ear to hear better, and the flower she had tucked there fell to the floor. As she leaned against him, wet from the shower, he replayed all the messages while she outlined the tattoo that ran down his naked shoulder. There were gentle reminders from friends he had barely seen since Emily, and a crisp few words from Malia asking if Professor Witt was still there.

"She is very worried that I will find a way to publish the journal, isn't she?"

"Not really."

"Then why is she so cold?"

"You are here - with me - like this. There has never been another woman here with me. You are *haole*. She is afraid. She knows that I will ask you to stay." Then Peter's voice came on, cool and tentative.

"This is a message for Dr. Emily Witt. This is Peter VanDyke calling. Em . . . the dean's office has been trying to find you about some *administrivia*. A meeting you missed last week? They finally called me, but I didn't know if I should give them this number or not. That must be Kamuela's voice on the machine. He sounds like I would like him. Anyway, they're dithering back here so you'd better give them a call. Hope you're ok. Better than ok. Aloha."

The meeting. She'd forgotten. Just as she'd forgotten the interim report. She hadn't looked at a calendar in . . . she couldn't even remember except that it seemed like the last time was the day she had changed the reservation for her return flight. She wasn't even sure where the calendar was but found it finally zipped into the side pocket of her laptop case. She had indeed missed a curriculum meeting and the deadline for her interim report on her research. It was the first deadline she had missed, ever, and the thought of it made her wince. This kind of license surely would have its price. It was already bedtime in New York, giving her a chance to fabricate a response that would justify her stay and disguise the real discoveries she had made. She'd e-mail it before bed and call first thing in the morning. Suddenly chilled, she stepped out of the circle of Kamuela's arm and found one of his shirts to put on.

Samuel would never remember how the dream began. There was only the ending to haunt him, the horror that had flung him awake and moaning into the arms of Napua, wet with fright. Within his dream there had been a pool of quiet water, but not their familiar bathing place. This one lay between gigantic boulders, green with lichen, and cold, full of eddies and froth swirling at the edge as he balanced on the slippery bank. The water reflected back the night sky with its crystal constellations, perhaps Orion, his dream self had thought. Stars dislodged themselves and shot across the heavens, first one, then several more, and then a blaze of meteoric transit that lit the night with an unnatural flash. And as above, so it was below. The current stiffened and rushed, filling the starry pool with shadows. Suddenly, in the way of dreams, there was a body floating by, a corpse in white trousers, a corpse impossibly white in the whiskey colored water, with auburn hair floating about the bobbing head, hair like his, and he fought to turn the body face-up, fearing it might be his own face that he would see, but try as he would, he could not move, his limbs weak with the fear of seeing himself, and then he struggled to pull the body over, but he was not strong enough, as if the corpse resisted, and then the water turned thick as syrup and full of maggots, fat white worms, and the churn of water thrust the dead man over and his arms reached out to Samuel.

He woke with the terror in him, fighting off Napua's hands until he recognized her voice and touch and threw himself upon her like a boy redeemed from death. He sobbed, gulping the air between them. She held him, curled and hiding, against her breast and belly, and slowly felt the cold dread go out of him and something warmer creep into his limbs. His mouth found her roundness and sucked hard, kindling them both. Then every shame dissolved and each took pleasure from the other, insistent, urgent, slipping beyond the desires and devices of their early loving into a passion so greedy that it frightened him slightly. They were all flesh and appetite, and nothing was forbidden. She took everything and gave him all, and he went with her until there was no place they had not touched, no sensation not reveled in, no hunger unappeased, and the wild, dark frenzy came on them, until the clutching and dissolving. They lay seared and breathless, a little raw.

The morning crept across the floor. Napua had not risen yet when he awoke, giving him light and leisure to look at his love. Usually she was up and bustling when he wakened, making a lover's game of his rising to look for her, and finding her already busy with the day. But now he saw her easy in her sleep, as if nothing was different, her brown arm flung across the covers, her palm open as if beckoning him again. Her mouth looked bruised, a little swollen. Then he remembered how it had been with her and slid out of the bed to dress quietly outside, taking a cigar he didn't light. He stretched in the early radiance of the day, feeling his back complain slightly, a reminder of the night. Before, he would have smiled at remembered pleasure with Napua, but now he stepped inside to look at her again, the familiar curves and color of her, and found something else. Now the mysteries of the night lay on her features. Napua was a creature who frightened him. She roused him too much.

It was a relief when she awoke and her smile banished his nagging discomfort with her. Then there was only the terror of last night's dream left.

My dreams are idle visions, says Napua. Native wisdom decrees that only the dreams of deepest sleep are prophetic and warrant interpretation. If you dream of dying, be assured that you will not actually die the next day or anytime soon, but whatever endeavor you had planned had best be postponed or abandoned – it is sure to fail. There is comfort and excuse in that system of theirs, but for myself, I mistrust it. Dreams have brought me warnings before, and I would heed this one. There is a familial curse from my mother's side, a tendency to die at the wrong time. An ancestor died after inheriting an English title and land to go with it. We die at the very moment when we could most benefit from not doing it. Thus am I inclined to fret about my nightmare.

Kamuela greeted Emily with the kind of rapture he always felt, a certain amazement that she was still there mingled with their shared delight at touching each other after absence. The weeks were hurtling past them, making every separation and reunion a rehearsal that added sweetness and passion to each.

When he tossed the canvas school bag down on the desk, the answering machine's insistent light caught him up with guilt. He would have preferred to listen to the messages without Emily close by, knowing that some of them brought the world into the narrow universe they had drawn around themselves. She glided to him and wrapped herself around him from behind, taking in the scent and heat of him so solid and substantial after a day of scholarly words and erudite imaginings.

The first message was a male voice, one of his friends, and Emily could not decode the rush of pidgin English. Though they rarely saw anyone at all, it always made her feel sad when a chance encounter in the market or on the beach erupted in a good-humored exchange that she could understand so little of. Kamuela did not translate for her or include her, and later when she would ask him who it was or what they had been laughing about, he would mostly shrug and say it was just this friend or that one he had gone to school with and they were only talking story, catching up. He had introduced her just once, to a cousin named Junior with skin weathered like jerky and a gap-toothed smile. He had looked at her with questions in his dark eyes as she stood there holding cartons of milk and guava nectar and a clutch of vegetables. "Emily," Kamuela had said. Just that. Then, "My *wahine*." Junior had only answered, "I heard." Neither of them had looked at her again. The rest was a blur of patois she only understood bits of. It was a relief - to all of them but for different reasons - when the two men embraced and parted. Kamuela always met his friends as if they had not seen one another in a very long time, and they parted tentatively as if they expected to meet again soon—realistic on this bit of sea-girt land.

Now the voice on the answering machine was insistent and urgent. It was about a party. Kamuela started to erase the message, and Emily reached to stop him. "A party? Do you want to go?"

"It's not important. A baby *luau*." It seemed that he didn't intend to explain what that meant as he usually did when some new feature of Hawaiian life caught her attention. Not this time.

"What's a *baby luau*?"

His shaman's voice, the one she rarely heard these days, answered. "When a baby makes one year, we have a party to celebrate. No one makes a party when a child is born, but at one year, there is a luau and presents, music, hula. It comes from the old time when many children didn't live to mark the first year."

"Whose baby?"

"My niece Pua's."

"We could go."

"I don't think you would like it." He could not tell her the reasons, so he made excuses. "It will be a very large party, and all my family, and local-style food. You might not have a good time."

"You don't want me to go? Fine. You go. Without me. I can find other things to do. *Haole* things. That's it, isn't it? You don't want to go and take me because I am *haole*. That's why you don't introduce me to your friends." The anger seemed to rise from some unmapped place in her. "You are ashamed. Ashamed of your white *wahine*." It made her sick and sad, but she believed that it was at least partly accurate.

"Not shamed—but scared. You might hate it, and it is part of me, and they might not be kind to you. They are proud to be who they are and don't understand you or you them. And if you hate it, will you love me less? I would not risk that." He still left the darkest reason unsaid. They stood apart in the evening air.

Emily couldn't stand the cold and the quiet. "That first day, when we went to the beach, and those boys looked so hard at us—together—I felt it. The women are the same. They don't want me here. They don't want me with you. They don't care who I am or what I am or that I love you. I am *haole*. That's all they see. That's why you won't go to the baby luau, isn't it? You are ashamed to be with a *haole*."

"You talk as if you do not know how much I love you. What it costs me to love you. My friends—the *ohana*—they do not understand yet."

Emily turned away from him. "I wish I was Hawaiian!" It was true. Sometimes as she watched the local women in their easy walk, proud and luscious, she was afraid that she would never feel such grace and belong to a place as thoroughly as they did. "Admit it – you do too."

"Never! You are Emily. Why would I wish you were not the woman I love? The woman I have waited for?"

"Because none of this would come between us."

"It does not need to now."

"But it has."

They were quiet for a long time, sitting apart on the *punene*. The night rain pelted the metal roof and bent the kiawe trees against the thin walls. There was no sound but the wet rasp of weather.

Kamuela almost whispered the question. "What if your family knew that you were here with me like this? That you loved me?"

There was no quick reply from her. "I don't know. Relief, maybe – that I had finally done something normal, fallen in love, but it won't matter to me what they think." Finally the cold between them gave way to their need to believe that love was more than enough.

"We can go." Resignation and anxiety edged his voice. "It's this Saturday. We will go, if you want to."

"You decide, but I want to go. I don't care how they look at me or through me or whatever."

When they held each other naked in the bed, Emily tried to lose herself in the familiar curves and hollows of him, wishing for the mindlessness of desire, but where their skins met, there was something new. She saw how his brown fingers insisted on her paleness. She held his darkest parts in her hand and wondered if she would love him like this if he were white. Or black. And then the question switched on itself, and she thought perhaps he would not love her quite this way if she was Hawaiian. They made love to each other carefully, missing the melt between them, keenly conscious of the planes where they touched, the cooler spaces where they didn't, the angle of spine and arch of muscle.

The white dress and sandals that she had decided to wear to the baby luau were all wrong. She had aimed for looking confidently comfortable with herself, tanned and sleekly happy, but the coarse sand of the beach caught against her soles as she walked toward the party, insinuating that she was dressed too obviously like a tourist. A *mu'umu'u* or even shorts and a shirt would have been a better choice. Under the rusty metal roof of the beach pavilion, the family was gathered in a swirl of balloons and crepe paper that rustled in the sunset breeze coming off the water. Emily had never heard a party from so far away, laughter sudden and full-bellied, a baby crying in the center of a solicitous circle of aunties and uncles, and the karaoke already begun. She hesitated at the edge of the commotion. A movement on the tin roof caught her eye. A rat skittered along the ridge and disappeared into the rafters.

Kamuela had planned their arrival for that moment between the languid talking story, the gathering of the clan, the tidal swirl of connecting and rejoicing in the family, and the moment that would open just before they bent to the business of eating. The niece Pua saw Kamuela, snatched the guest of honor from the young man who was cradling him, and came barefoot across the rough cement floor like a temple dancer bearing a precious offering. "Uncle Kam! You have hardly seen my boy!" She pressed the little one to him. Emily was not surprised at how knowingly he held the baby or at the child's adoring gaze into Kamuela's eyes. She turned toward the mother expectantly as Kamuela gestured, "Pua, this is Emily." The mother shifted between her manners and her inclination, almost holding a hand out to Emily self-consciously as if it was something she had seen in a movie, but then quickly putting her cheek next to Emily's instead with a quiet "Aloha." Emily returned the greeting in kind. There was a bustle as the rest of the family noticed their arrival and called out their greetings over the heads of one another until the grandmother of the baby took over, clapping for everyone's attention.

When it was quiet, Pua asked Kamuela to say the blessing. With so many elders around, it seemed odd to Emily, and she planned to ask her lover why he was chosen. Someone gripped Emily's hand, the one

Kamuela was not holding fast and close, as a circle formed. Someone else slipped a green *maile lei* around his neck, and he began to pray the blessing in Hawaiian. Bent heads nodded at things Emily did not understand. Then the gentle candences broke into English and then a loud "*amene*!" and rowdy "*kau kau*! Eat!"

Emily held back as the family pressed past her, Kamuela giving her silent direction with his palm at her back. In the swarm, there must have been some protocol that she could not discern, so she waited. His aunt Malia pushed by them with a nod. Beside her drifted the loveliest Hawaiian woman Emily had seen—tall, like Malia, with a breadth of shoulder and hip and small, supple waist that gave her graceful step an imperial quality. The arch of her neck was unbendingly regal. Kamuela pressed Emily forward into the line that wound around the food tables. Malia and the younger woman were quickly beyond earshot as Kamuela joked with cousins across mounds of sticky rice and pots of *poi*, platters of roast pig and *laulau*, pausing to tell her what each dish was and suggest she try it - or not - according to his intimacy with her hungers and tastes.

There was no moment of hesitation when Kamuela led them to seats at one of the long paper-covered tables. He had clearly thought it through as he watched the crowd and then negotiated their way to places across from the man she remembered as Junior. Kamuela introduced them again, reminding her of their meeting in the grocery, and then included the blonde wife who sat beside him, JoJo. The men talked fishing and ate, but mostly ate. JoJo leaned across the table toward Emily and asked where in New York she was from. Kamuela hadn't mentioned New York in the introductions, and Emily knew that these two were not the only family members who had heard about his *haole wahine* from the so-called "mainland."

The karaoke began again making it impossible to really talk across the table. Kamuela had to lean into her shoulder to explain something or other that was happening or identify someone who passed by. The young mother wandered from table to table, passing the baby to anyone who asked. Behind her, the young man hovered in attendance, his hands always touching Pua or the baby or both. He seemed younger than Pua and besotted with mother and child, cocooned in her maternal eroticism, his face the mix of many races that local people wore so well, a democratic beauty. Emily asked about him, the father.

"The baby's father? He's over there," pointing to a local boy lounging against a post just within the circle of light, laughing with the other young men. "They were not married. The boy with Pua, he is her new boyfriend." Emily studied the clutch of dark boys at the edge of the party, their quiet talk and shared laughter, dressed uniformly and formally in slim trousers and flowered shirts instead of the usual surf shorts and "attitude" t-shirts. As if Kamuela anticipated disapproval, he added, "To quote my ancestor, 'It is not immoral to create a human species, with or without a ceremony.' "

Junior picked at Kamuela's sleeve and nodded over

his shoulder. Malia and the beauty swept down on them. The younger woman spoke to Kamuela without greeting or preamble. "You were missed at the fund-raiser last weekend." There was something hidden in the comment that Emily could not decipher though she felt how it insisted on a certain intimacy with him. Kamuela half-turned to her instead of answering directly.

"Emily, this is Lokelani. *Loke* is head teacher at the Hawaiian language immersion school." Loke continued to look only at him. "Emily is a teacher, too," returning the look but touching Emily's arm, "from New York."

"I have heard. Aloha." Loke turned away and smiled graciously at no one, a practiced beauty. She and Malia moved on. She had made sure that everyone at the luau would understand how Emily had been dismissed. Even though Loke chanced some censure for her lack of aloha, it was a small risk considering that Emily was not just *haole* but mainland *haole*, a visitor, and not from the islands despite the gossip about her being born here.

The cake was about to be cut with the flourish usually - at least in New York - reserved for wedding cakes. Just beyond the center of everything, Malia presided, almost eclipsing the baby and grandparents. Beside her, Loke stood in attendance. Emily wanted to ask Kamuela about her but hesitated, merely watching her as she and Malia very publicly ignored her and Kamuela as well. Emily spoke across the table to JoJo and the blonde suggested that the two of them go to find the *lua*. Inside the toilet at the back of the beach pavilion, JoJo lit up a hand-rolled cigarette that Emily knew was not tobacco and began to chatter through the swinging door. "Listen - don't let it get to you. They treated me the same way, at first. Junior used to get mad. But after awhile, they started talking to me, called me by name instead of '*Junior's wahine*.' It's not that they don't like you. They just think we're aliens, you know? They think they don't know what to say to us, like we speak a foreign language or something. It'll get better. Except for Loke."

"Who?"

"Loke – *Lokelani* - the one who is always with Auntie Malia. She's just never going to like you, you know?"

"Why not?"

"You're kidding! Kam didn't tell you?" Emily felt a clutch in her chest. "Loke and Kamuela were supposed to get married. Years ago. The *ohana* has just always sort of expected it, but when they got to the right age, he refused. Everybody kept pushing them together, and Loke wants him, but he told Junior he doesn't love her."

Emily pushed down the important questions that her heart wanted to ask.

"Why is it so important to the family? the *ohana*?" she corrected herself.

"Loke is from one of the old *ali'i* families. Practically royalty. They have some land. And she's almost full-on Hawaiian. It's about the Homelands too, Junior says."

"I don't understand."

"Hawaiian Homelands. You have to be fifty percent Hawaiian blood or more to qualify for the land, and if your children aren't at least that, the land goes back to the government when you die - your family can't have it." JoJo sucked smoke, coughed and spoke in a hoarse half-whisper holding the smoke in. "That land Aunty Malia has up on the mountain? Did he take you up there? Kamuela will get it someday, but his kids would lose it, if he married a *haole*—you—for instance."

Emily pushed out of the stall and leaned at the sink. The water was cold on her hands, soothing. "Well, the *ohana* need not worry about that. I am going back to New York soon. "

"Yeah, you're a teacher or something."

"A professor. English." Emily hated the imperious tone that cut the soft air, but she didn't know any other way to be defensive. JoJo shrugged and drew deeply on her cigarette, knowing the chance for some girl talk had vanished. It didn't feel like a loss to either of them as they walked back to the *luau* in separate silences.

The music had shifted from amped-up karaoke to a pair of ukeleles and one guitar accompanying whoever would sing along. The men strummed between songs, conferring loudly over what to play next, then called out a title in Hawaiian. Two cousins who had hastily tied sarongs over their shorts kicked off their rubber slippers and began to dance a fast hula, laughing over their shoulders at the musicians, winking dramatically as they swayed, dipped and turned. The crowd laughed and applauded encouragement. Another song began immediately, and another of the girl cousins and the new grandmother joined in. Slower than the others, this song seduced Junior into singing along. Plaintive, sensuous, like a long goodbye, the women danced his song, barely smiling, making love to the night air and the music. Then there was another hula of quick steps and much laughter, the unmistakable gestures of sex and teasing, and two of the younger men joined in with cousins they had known since "small kid time," dancing a flirtation that was only hula fun. On and on it went until everyone was sweaty and laughing, and the new grandmother sat down tired while the rest kept dancing.

Malia stepped to the edge of the darkness beyond the pavilion and leaned to whisper something into the ear of one of the ukelele players. He passed it on, and at the end of the next song there was a long pause. When one of the musicians called out a new hula, the dancers moved to the side.

Loke rose from her seat at the far edge of the party and walked slowly toward the center of the open space, *keiki* and dogs skittering out of her way. She left her shoes and unpinned her hair, shaking it out until it made a dark cataract down her back. Lifting the hem of her Hawaiian dress slightly, gathering its drifts of bright flowers in her fingertips, she nodded once to the musicians and began to dance. The sweep of her long arms and sway of her curves mesmerized them all. She danced as if no one else existed, mimicking the trees, moving against the music like water against shore. Superb, fine, full of grace, she was more than herself. She was the goddess dancing, and everyone knew it. Kamuela stirred beside Emily, then stood. Barefoot, he danced toward Loke, then behind her, shadowing every movement of hers with his own. Together, whispers apart, they moved with the pulse of the hula, slow eddies of dance, his body arching perfectly to hers. The dark lines of his tattoo rippling from beneath his sleeve and shorts gave Emily something besides their matched beauty to look at, something to cling to. She had never known him as he was then except in bed. He was all smooth sinew and muscle, holding himself in thrall to the woman dancing, worshipping all that she was in those moments. Bare feet swept the cement floor, knees bent to weave the curves of hip and arms together, arcing into patterns of seduction and goodbye. Loke never looked at Kamuela, and he looked at no one but her. Emily suspected that they had danced this hula many times together. When it was over, she applauded along with everyone else, but formally, without heart. The two dancers left the floor without speaking to each other. Their eyes never met. Kamuela took Emily's hand as he settled back into his seat at the picnic table and pressed it hard against his thigh. She felt a quiver of muscle there.

Later at home, he took a worn blue notebook down from the shelf and read to her. One hand moved continuously over her skin as his voice softened around the translated English lyrics of the hula he had danced.

"When the rain drums loud on the leaf
It makes me think of my love;
It whispers into my ear,
Your love – your love – she is near.

Thou art the end of my longing,
The crown of evening's delight,
When I hear the cock blithe crowing
In the middle watch of the night.
This way is the path for thee and me,
A welcome warm at the end.
I waited long for thy coming,
And found thee in the waft of the breeze."

Emily more than heard the lyrics. The meanings, revealed by his voice and touch, the rich enchantment of words, stirred her, reminding her that it was just this – this way that words moved her into herself and beyond – it was what she had loved, why she had chosen English as a profession in the first place, but profession had replaced passion when long training and scholarly necessity had all but strangled the love out of her.

In bed later he moved beside her, over her, as he had danced, and she understood what the hula had meant, and knew that he had danced for her.

When Peter didn't answer his phone, Emily realized she had not accounted for the six hour discrepancy between where she was and Buffalo. It was more than just time zones, she knew. It rattled her to feel how completely she had adapted to "Hawaiian time," the actual hours as well as the Polynesian tendency to do things "whenever."

Since she and Peter were the last two people they knew who didn't carry cell phones, she had to strain to remember his office number at the campus. He answered on the first ring, sounding crisp and impatient.

"Peter. It's Emily."

"So it is. How wonderful that it's you and not – you know – one of *them*."

"Your students?"

"Them too, but I meant our colleagues." She didn't respond. "How are you, Em?" More silence. "Em?"

"I need to ask you something – do you have a minute?"

"Of course, and more if you want. What's up? Is it the Twain material?"

"Not really. Not at all, actually. The work is going along fine, and the *ohana* – the family – seems more tolerant of me, of my being here."

"So what's wrong?"

"It's just, well, just now when I called you, I forgot to calculate the time difference. Just forgot. It's not like me to forget things like that – and that meeting I missed. I don't even know for sure what day it is! And yesterday, I was sitting near the beach just watching how palm trees move."

"Sounds like you're on vacation. That's not a bad thing. I know you probably never had one before, but you have heard about them – vacations – right?"

"It's more than that. Last night, I saw myself reflected

in a window in town and didn't recognize who it was. I don't look like me. And yet I wished that I looked like Loke, Kamuela's cousin – so beautiful and graceful and comfortable in her skin. I don't want to be *haole* – sorry, I mean white. How can it be so easy to give up my self like that?" She listened to the electronic pulse in the line. "Remember what you said to me about going native?"

"I was only kidding, Em."

"Well, I see how it happens. Twain did it. Life here is just so damned beautiful and gentle and seductive. People here go around smiling, enjoying their days. Even rain – they call it liquid sunshine and don't worry about getting wet – and people walk outside to look for rainbows. Nothing is dark or hurried or dangerous. Even Kamuela says there is nothing to fear here. Nothing but forgetting who you were before you came."

"How does Kamuela figure into this?"

Emily took a breath the way her lover did before speaking deep truth. "I love him. And it isn't just the sex. It makes no sense. I love him. And I don't want to be away from him. He is so present, right here in each moment. Being near him is like being plugged into some transcendent something – I don't even have words for it. And that's not like me either. I want to stay with him. But what about Professor Emily Witt? What happened to her?"

"Alchemy of love, Em. It changes us or else it isn't love."

"What happens when my time here is done, and I am back in Buffalo, and classes begin, and I have to put my clothes back on, and . . . "

"Whoa! What are you really afraid of?"

"Not being able to be her again - Professor Emily Witt."

"You're not supposed to. You know things you didn't know before, and you get to bring them back with you. It's the mythic quest, Em. You have captured the key that transforms dross into gold, and when you return, you bring it with you."

"And Kamuela?"

"That's up to him, isn't it? This I know: as much as you have changed, he has as well. That's how love works."

"And if this new Emily doesn't fit in back in Buffalo? What if this new Emily just won't translate?"

"She might not. Remember who you left behind here besides me? Victims of arrogance and tenure. Bored, unproductive people who dislike their students and themselves. But Hawai'i isn't going anywhere. It will still be there. You can go back. It has started to sound like you might prefer there anyway."

"But there's tenure in Buffalo."

"And not much else, is there? Not that tenure isn't worth something. We have to make a living, and it's an easy gig once you get that security. But what you said about Kamuela being the present – can you just be there right now? Stop worrying about what's next and just be with what is?"

"You're teaching Thoreau right now, aren't you?"

"Yes, but I learned that from Ben's dying, not from Thoreau."

"Thank you, Peter."

"You're welcome, girlfriend. What are you going to do now?"

"It's 4:14 AM here, and I am going to slip back into bed with Kamuela and wait for dawn."

"Try sleeping."

"That too."

"Call anytime. I'm here no matter where you are."

"I know, and I love you for it. Aloha."

May 18

The dream haunts me still. Every vexing detail seems to invite interpretation, and I fear it foretells my end if I remain here. It is not yet a decade since that prophetic dream I had of brother Henry laid out in a coffin in the sitting room - the flowers, the casket balanced on two chairs - and how it all came to pass exactly as I dreamed it. For one who dreams so little, I dream too much and such cataclysmic visions! I would rather have my nightmares in the daytime. This new night horror taints my delight in the days. I wake to misgivings in the moonlight and even the night's splendor and Napua beside me cannot deliver me from the dread the dream has left behind. By day, Napua and Maui sustain me, but at night a mouldering, morbid, macabre terror enthralls me - a mortal fear of dying in that river too - deceased, departed, dead and gone like the leper—nameless, obscure, with neither marker nor mourners.

Mortality demands a sense of one's destiny, and mine lies elsewhere.

I have been called to literature, though it be only of the low order of literary comedy or even reportage. It is my strongest suit, my little gift, and I must follow it and cease this trifling. Eden offers no subject for a writer. The true source of comedy is sorrow – bliss has no humor in it. I am not ripe for paradise yet. It is no doubt some flaw in my character, this vulgar ambition, but it propels my vain self and I cannot remain here. There is too much still to tell, imperfect lies, I suppose, and a truth so beautiful few will believe it, a fact here and there, and underneath it all, this aloha, this woman, this land, this stolen season of rapture and ruin.

But for now, I surrender to the blandishments of the world.

May 21

I am back here in Wailuku late today. Napua is with me. We came most of the way by outrigger canoe, arranged by Lono. His enthusiasm for my departure prompts some speculation about his friendship toward us – he seems too eager for my leave-taking. We are staying out of the way to keep our arrival clandestine, going about separately until we find each other again tonight at a place she has secured for us. I suspect it is too late to save her reputation, and my own is of no account, but her sentiments on the matter are no trifle.

I have booked passage for tomorrow on the schooner Ka Mo'i back to Oahu. The fellow at the ticket office told me the date, though the full moon was all I needed for calendar. The office was a hive - a great many people are going to Honolulu now as the legislature is reconvening. Having missed the King's grand opening of Parliament on the 25th, I suppose I must be present for this spectacle. I suspect it is about like all other such gatherings, and that isn't saying much that's complimentary. Politics hold little charm for me just now.

There's a rumor on the waterfront that Princess Victoria Kamamalu has died or is about to, but I give it little credence – the circumstances are too mysterious and her highness is known for her vigor and prowess, especially in the private chamber. Haole gossips whisper that she maintains a harem of 36 strapping young men, keeping them all employed with her appetites. I dare not ask Napua about it.

The streets of this port are full of characters – hustlers, stevedores, soldiers, ministers, murderers, bawds and belligerents. No saloon has presented itself though. The waterfront lacks the roughness of Lahaina, but there is still about this place the mood and manner of Mississippi River towns. The byways teem with faces of every degree of darkness, a white face in their midst seeming unwholesome, ghastly, marked by the sun's blush rather than enhanced by it. A white complexion is a poor counterfeit of Adam's. The Creator himself was no doubt a dark beauty and made the first man in His likeness!

After a week's worth of asking, I at last found the only reputable barber in Kahului, a New Yorker with surgical tendencies, judging by the way he brandished the razor as he brooded aloud over the impending parliamentary debacle in Honolulu. Despite that, I am well-shorn, trimmed and haberdashed again. I fear I am a Samsonite, thus undone. Napua has stitched the hem of my duster up to better suit my stature. She will hardly recognize her "Maka."

I watched the ticket agent write "Clemens, Samuel," and I signed the manifest. I hardly know who that is now. Having left that old identity somewhere by a waterfall in the vicinity of east Maui, I wonder if I can ever wear it again to advantage. "Maka." The sages have said that travel begets new thought, but it seems to me it has birthed a new man as well, one who comes with just a small satchel of expectation and an idea or three about our brown friends, these fellow savages. You can bring back all sorts of communicable and infectious things from distant places if you are not careful, love and tolerance among them.

Napua and I both pretend, as one is tempted to do with the dying, that there will be another time ahead for us. Imagination fails when I consider the moment of parting from her. Resolve may too. She will not try to hold me here, that much is clear. Her dignity forbids it. She expects me to go. I fear that I can never be as good as she is, not half enough to carry off this farewell, my aloha being so sharpened with anguish that somehow I have dishonored her. Dishonored and abandoned. I have dreamed of honor but had no practice at it and am entirely uncertain how to behave.

Perhaps I have got it wrong. She has loved me but briefly, a months's dalliance by Hawaiian reckoning. In a month's time, she may love another, Lono perhaps, and "Maka" will be eclipsed.

Travelers bustled at the wharf while native stevedores and the occasional cowboy steered through the disarray of crates and baggage. Samuel had begun to be gone before he actually left. It was always so. Once the choice to depart is made, the going begins. Increments of farewell, gathering those other clothes that one will need, packing up the heart, a certain longing to be gone, a bustle of regret. It was as broiling hot as August in New York without the steam – he made a note to himself to remember the comparison. A cow boat was about to leave with its bleating cargo blessedly downwind as he left the packet line office and looked hard for Lono. He searched each visage, surprised that now each one bore its stamp of individuality. Where only a month before he had seen simply "Kanaka," he recognized today the subtle differences of feature that the native people had in their broad, open faces - here a fullness of mouth that was more than his beloved's, and there a cheekbone not as high and wide as Lono's. Lono himself appeared momentarily from nowhere, materializing from the ether, and joined Samuel, leading him through the streets of Kahului and into a shaded by-way. Napua waited, a study in stoicism. She welcomed him into the cooler dampness of the borrowed bungalow where they would spend their last night together.

The next morning, there was a shuddering rupture as they pulled away from each other. He had extracted her promise that she would not go down to the wharf with him when the *Ka Mo'i* departed. Theirs would be a private farewell in the dim garden, no witnesses but Lono and their two hearts. Napua waited, once again shrouded in the shapeless calico dress of the missionaries, but her hair cascaded around her in the errant breeze. When he held her, he felt her heat and sorrow. How could a day be so beautiful when there was such a storm inside him, he wondered. What kind of paradise so ignores the state of a man's heart and soul? Napua laid a lei of ti leaf on his shoulders and tucked one of the sacred leaves into his pocket for safe travel. Lono looked away rather than see her hurting. She pressed a small package into Samuel's hand, telling him it was awa, a cure for the seasickness if the crossing was rough. She had given him all she could of everything. She whispered into his shoulder, "Jehovah and all the gods go with you," and then "Hoi hou – come back."

The pier was a man's domain where the brisk industry of inter-island business was presided over by a few dark-suited gentlemen with cigars, ranchers in mud-spattered garb, and a Chinese merchant counting his bundles in insistent Cantonese. Trade winds cooled the fretting crowd, but when the wind dropped, the blazing sun seared them. A horse too close to the edge whinnied and lurched when a rat slid behind a box into darkness, and a few Kanakas laughed at the fracas and the sweating haoles. Clemens stood apart from the rush, staring off toward Hana. The red earth was lacerated for the new sugar cane planting. His heart hurt like that, he thought, and turned to look back at the harborfront once more before stepping aboard. There he leaned heavily against the gunwale and studied the water below that sucked and surged and made a hollow slap against the vessel - fish-less water, befouled by all that commerce.

A somewhat shabby fellow in a felt hat sidled next to him at the rail.

"Clemens?" he asked, certain of the answer. A nod of assent was all Samuel could manage. "Thought so. Weston, George Washington Weston, at your service," with an obsequious bow. Clemens turned aside to look back one last time. The timbers of the steamer creaked. The whistle sounded the departing call, and they began to slip away from shore. All lines were cast off until there was nothing visible holding him to the island. At the edge of the crowd back there, Napua appeared from a shadow and stood, one hand raised motionless. Her lips, so dear to him, seemed to call out "Aloha" and "Maka." The expanse of murky harbor water between them grew as the vessel picked up speed, and Samuel judged the depth and distance and thought that he could swim it and would rather drown in trying than endure this awful tearing at his heart.

He put one foot on the gangway opening and leaned, and looked again at Napua growing smaller with each moment and measured the distance with his heart and launched himself into the growing gulf between the ship and shore.

The felt-hat man grabbed for him, clawed at his shoulders for a handhold and dragged him back.

"Thought you were going to fall! Lucky I was close by. Staring at the water does that to a man sometimes. He loses his balance."

Clemens sought the figure of Napua again and found her, hands pleading, but yes or no, he could not tell. She turned into Lono's embrace, and he led her away, disappearing into the dimness between the sun-glazed buildings of Kahului.

Kamuela was still at the church working when Emily sat down in the shade of the kiawe trees behind his house to read Napua's pages of diary. She had worked over Clemens's journal itself very slowly, meticulously noting the dates and themes, cross-referencing, saving the fascicle of Napua's dated pages and the unopened letters until now without thinking why. She and Kamuela had seen almost no one since the baby luau, staying secluded in the blue house by the water, recovering the lost mystery of their early love. Ordinary time receded again. Now there was a cautious tenderness between them, anticipating their parting and suspending their mutual need for some kind of promise.

The pages smelled of maile, just like Clemens's journal, having been put away for generations in the fragrant leaves, renewed often by whichever member of the ohana held the bundle. Emily knew the paper was too brittle to open the pages wide and flat, held too tightly by the antique stitches along the edge. Similar bundles from the hands of genteel 19th century women were kept in museum vaults and library drawers all over the mainland, but for Napua, there were no satin ribbons or colorful paper covers for binding. There was only the thick paper torn from a ledger, pages etched with a schoolgirl's smooth handwriting.

April 16, 1866 – Divine Providence has kept me safe through this day. Rain overtook us and we hastened to get to our night's refuge. Had Mr. Clemens been a better horseman, we would have been caught, but his slowness kept us on the ridge above Kaumahina gulch just long enough that the water did not catch us at the bottom and take us out to sea. We lost one bundle and the contents of the saddlebag when his horse lost its footing, but Mr. Clemens seems to have lost little that he values. He does not complain. He has cigars and whiskey. We have made a shelter upslope above the cave and will stay until the rain ends and the rivers are gone again. He says it was I who saved his life and will not listen when I tell him that it was God.

April 18, 1866 – He sleeps now. In the quiet I will write this so that I will not forget. When Mr. K. engaged my brother to guide this haole to Hana, we hid our laughter as we had when we first saw him in the street – this Mr. Clemens in his long coat that flaps about his legs like a sail and drags in the dust. Mr. Clemens with the ehu hair. Mr. Clemens who spoke with such a flurry of hands and rasping voice that we thought him a drunkard. Mr. Clemens. Samuel.

He wears a good lauhala hat from Honolulu but calls it "my panama." It is too large for him, and fits low on his head, nearly resting on his brow. It hides the laughter that is so often in his eyes. The coat that he wears hangs to his ankles like muumuu. It is of pale cloth like sailor's canvas and covers him completely. He is lost inside his clothes. When he rides, the coat drags and bunches, ever getting in the way. Though it is unseemly, the girls in town wondered what he wore beneath the strange garment. If I had my sewing things with me, I would cut it off for him and hem it to a proper length.

April 19 - Samuel is never quiet, except when he eats or sleeps or smokes. He chatters and wants to know everything, all about the sugar and pineapple, and when he is done asking, he talks about himself and America. He likes the sound of his voice, or perhaps he is afraid of the quiet. I hardly ever need to speak or find a moment to. He asks the name of everything he notices and writes it down in the little book he carries. Words flow out of him like stream water after rain. He has an antic spirit though, brimming with mischief. He is like a boy. When he talks, his arms go every which way. His Christian name is Samuel, yet I see none of that ancient wisdom in him. His brows are like brushes, hiding his merry eyes that shine sometimes with the color of water in a deep pool. They give his countenance a guarded aspect, combined with the great bush of mustache beneath his nose. And below that, always a cigar and smoke curling around his head like the halo in the pictures at church. He chatters and throws his arms in gestures for accompaniment to everything he says and sometimes he walks with a certain indirectness. Even in his sleep he walks sometimes and wanders. I lead him back to his sleeping place and he wakes without remembering. I will give him awa to drink to keep his spirit safe in his body.

April 20, 1866 He sleeps. When he is quiet, I see him clearly. His hair is not so wild now, but still it has the fire in it. His skin today is red as well, burnt by the sun. Now in the cool shade here beside the stream, he has rolled his sleeves in the way the reverend does when he works, and I can see the whiteness of skin above his wrist where sunlight has not touched him. He is so ungainly, foolish in his wild gait, his head too big for his shoulders.

He writes often in the little book, whetting the pencil point with his tongue that pokes out beneath the brush of his mustache. He is quite hairy, even for a hoale man.

And small. He writes and talks. I never knew a man to talk so much, even more than the missionaries. He wants to know the name of everything and why things are and what they mean. It is easy now to make him laugh. One who did not know him would think him a drunkard, but it is only that he rushes eagerly from excitement to excitement. He speaks, then pauses, looks to me, as if I am there to give him a response, some answer, the way the missionaries do in church, but there is nothing to say and he looks disappointed. I suppose he is used to more conversation.

April 22 The moon is full again. The pool above our refuge – "the raft" he calls it – is where we bathe. He has learned to wash his clothes there as well, and we take our ease in the heat of mid-day as well. I cover myself, seeing how he looks away. Shamed, I think. Perhaps he is mahu and does not desire women. Yet I believe I see wela in his eyes sometimes when he looks at me. Merry Maka, with eyes sometimes blue or sea-gray or even green – with his changing mood or a trick of the light – looking, always, for something.

April 23, 1866 – Lono came today. How he found us, he did not tell. I think he does not like Maka. When he begins to talk, Lono looks away to the sea or disappears. But I know he stays near. He brings a little news. In Hana they do not look for us, thinking Samuel has changed his plan and gone elsewhere, maybe back to Honolulu. In Kahului they probably think we went to

Hana and beyond. No one seeks us, everyone believing we are somewhere else. Lono has not told anyone otherwise, I am sure. He is quiet, always watching. The music is his only conversation. How restful his silence is to me sometimes.

April 27, 1866 – Lono stayed with us this night. He played the hano long into the twilight, songs of love that I remember from those other nights together. Maka hardly seems to notice Lono's attentions to me, and it is just as well. Lono brought him cigars and news, to please me. There is a man on horseback searching for Maka. He has gone as far as Hana asking for "Mr. Clemens." Lono has promised to tell my mother that I am safe and well to relieve her mind, but she will be angry when she discerns that I am with the haole in this way.

April 30 Lono came again last night. He knows how it is with Maka and me. He spoke of it and asked me why. He has loved me so long and is a good man. I cannot tell him what I do not understand. The love I bear for Lono is from our childhood time and when we were older, when we shared those first stirrings and learned our love lessons together and then made our commitment to the church together. I did not know this other kind of love.

May 10, 1866 How far from righteousness this love has led me! The man who seeks Maka found us, and I told him a lie, a vile untruth about my father and the mai pake and now I tremble to think that love has prompted me to such dangerous deception. May the gods not hear the lie, or hearing it, know that it was love that told it, and not punish my father by making the lie a fact. A man like Maka who speaks much must surely now and then utter an untruth – it is to be expected in such a torrent of words. It is the haole way, I think. And his god does not listen, he says. I know that all gods hear and hear all, and I fear the fulfillment of my words.

May 14, 1866 Maka sleeps until the sun is up. The cool time after first light is mine alone. I rise and make my prayers and write a little here. I begin to see that I have left the path of righteousness and write too much of Maka and less of the Lord. It is my bleeding time and there is none. I could take the herbs and bring it on, but I do not want to.

May 22 Maka left today. I have seen the felt-hatted man in the street and know that he has found the Mr. Clemens that he sought. Maka left behind his diary and a letter and more. He does not know. Perhaps the child will not persist with me. Lono is here with me still. He comforts me. He has asked if I will marry him now. Maka will not return, he says. Perhaps he is right. We are leaving for Lahaina tomorrow.

June 22, 1866 Today there is a letter from Maka sent from Honolulu. It smells of cigar. I cannot bear to open it for I know what it says, how he promises to come again. He wishes it was so. Perhaps he tells me he is coming on Tuesday. I still do not want to read it. I would not breathe until Tuesday, if I knew. Better to see him walking down the street to me and be surprised. Or maybe he upbraids me for not writing letters to him. There is nothing I have not said except to tell him there will be a keiki, and he will know that if he comes again. I will not read the letter. It is enough to hold it and know that it passed from his hand only a few days ago.

July 16, 1866 It is Mahealani again, the full moon, Maka's moon. It comforts me that somewhere beyond the horizon, he is under the same moon, feeling the passage of the months. I need no such reminder. My opu begins to grow. The Reverend Mr. Finney will marry us if we do it quickly before I look too hapai. He is angry with me, and disappointed in Lono, believing he is this keiki's father. It is just as well. And if this little one has ehu hair, what of it? Rare is the child of Pele's fire and precious as any babe. My mother has gone to the minister and wept, begging for a wedding. Lono is happy at last, and I resolve to be.

December 23, 1866 This keiki will be born soon, but I am not afraid. This little one is full of antic spirit like the father, always tossing and heaving inside me. Lono and I wed together on the first Tuesday in August, and this is my last page for Maka and our child, a son for Maka. I had a dream. Many years from now, the ancestors will bring another haole here to our ohana, one who will want to know about Maka, and this book of his will give her all she seeks. They will know her by the way she comes like a white bird filling the sky. In the future is our past – I ka wa mamua, ka wa mahope.

Emily closed the fascicle and realized that the sun had shifted enough to shine on a patch of her thigh that now burned. She wondered how long she had been reading and weeping and if Kamuela would be home soon.

He stepped into the back doorway as if he had been going through the house searching for her, rehearsing her absence, relieved to find her still there. "What's this? Tears?"

"Napua . . . her love . . . what it cost her," Emily sniffed.

"It always does."

"He never came back. And she just went on."

"Lovers only kill themselves in literature." He sat beside her on the grass mat and breathed the smells of her. "The rest of us just go on. It is better to live for love than die for it, I think."

Emily held the three unopened letters, looking carefully at the stamps, the marks on the old vellum, the scribble of address, and finally the bold SLC on the back of each one. "I can't open them."

Kamuela imagined some scholarly reason. "Why not?"

"Napua never did. How can I?"

"I will do it for you. I have some right, perhaps. Do

you want me to do it?"

"I don't know. Yes. And no."

"You have read everything else, why not these?"

"Because she didn't. Because she could love and let go like that."

He slid the edge of his penknife between the edges of the first envelope where the old adhesive had long ago dried up. "Let me. He was my ancestor." He began to read them to her, not mimicking the fractious cadences of Clemens's style but recasting the elder Samuel's voice in the velvet of the younger.

May 25, 1866.

Beloved flower,

I am back in Honolulu where the streets are buzzing over the death of Princess Victoria Kamamalu . Much *pilikia* *about the funeral too, and whether it will have the operatic grief of Hawaiian tradition or the high church ritual of the Anglicans. Whispers everywhere that it was a botched attempt to rid her royal self of an unwanted keiki. One hears of such things in the alleys of San Francisco, but here where children are so beloved, it seems a particular atrocity, a remnant of the monarchy's lust for incest that your missionary friends blessedly erased.*

The passage back to Oahu was long owing to the reluctant seas. I might have taken it for a sign that even the Pacific held me back from leaving you. Alone under the moonlight, reclining on deck, awaiting sleep, I was denied the soft refreshing slumber that comes to those both weary and innocent. I was sentenced to a fitful night of anxious dream and waking sorrows, wishing I had never left you. The night was one long dark lament.

The felt-hat man was aboard. He's a <u>*Union*</u> *man, sent by the newspaper, as I suspected. He won't let me out of his sight. I expect I will have to take the steamer to Hawaii Island to escape him.*

I am adrift. I have given up light and compass, knowing only one direction, one place – you. The rest of the world is a sunless forest where I must wander awhile, always holding fast to the image of you, my home, that endless summer landscape with my flower in its center, lovely and lonesome as a dreamy Sunday. I have always been hankering to get back on the great river that I told you of, but henceforth I shall only long to be there in the green with you. Though I have left Maui, it will never leave me. You are my beacon in this sojourn back to the realm of darkness.

Your Maka

Emily made notes as Kamuela began reading the second letter.

June 22, Honolulu.

Beloved Blossom,

I am rushing to get this missive on the next steamer. You may have heard of the wreck of the Hornet in waters near the Galapagos Islands with eleven men surviving forty-three days at sea. One lone lifeboat came to shore and safety at Lapahoehoe on Hawaii Island. Having written all night to get a piece off on the next boat to California, I will likely "scoop" that story, as we say in the newspaper trade. There's great drama in it – cannibalism and all. Providence has brought me here in the path of the story and it's mine to capitalize on if only I can get the story into print first!

It has been a trial. I returned from Hawaii Island sick and sore and kept to my bed for days since, but Burlingame has been a great help, having me transported down to the hospital to see the survivors. I am on the mend, you see. The only part of me that aches now is my heart.

Your Maka

Emily brought them each a tall passionfruit drink from the kitchen and settled on the *punene* beside him again. Kamuela drank the tart *lilikoi* and read on.

August 1866, San Francisco.

Dearest Napua,

'Home again' – so my brother Orion and my creditors say – but no, not home. In prison again, and all my sweet freedom gone. The city is cramped and filthy, gritty with toil and business anxiety and fruitless cares and useless necessities. I am weary but determined to make good here. The Hawaii Letters from the Union have brought me some small celebrity, and I am going to ride that wave out of financial worry and back again to you, beloved girl. The Union has given me a tidy

bonus, and the Hornet story will do well toward paying off the creditors.

I hope that our friend Lono is with you and taking good care.

I have hired a hall and commenced my career as a lecturer, going on the stage to talk the rest of my way to solvency. Not as Maka, but as "Mark Twain." Can you imagine that people will come to listen to me when they might be at prayer meeting or the morgue? But they do come and they pay for it! I will tell them about Hawaii, but not all of it, and make them laugh until the coins jingle out of their pockets! Beneath each word from me will be the one unspoken – Napua.

Another frog story is percolating in me, about to erupt. These days it is no more trouble for me to write than it is to lie, and my dearest, you know well how effortless that is unless I have your sweet countenance to rein me in!

Between the writing and the talking, I will pay off the credit vultures and get my passage back to Maui.

You can write to me at the paper, dear. Any missive from that darling hand of yours would be a treasure – just a line or two, even.

With my deepest aloha, Maka

October 7, 1866

Dear Flower,

I am riding a firecracker since the lecture, a real 'Nantucket sleigh ride'. Enclosed is one of the reviews, from the Bulletin. He spelled my old name wrong, but not the one that mattered! Two thousand men and women who had no better judgment and nothing more charitable to do with their money paid to hear "Mark Twain."

I shall soon be as slick in my vernacular as a preacher in his pulpit. I have added a distinctly Hawaiian touch – the pause. Nothing so captivates a listener as a stretch of silence – it's all anticipation then.

The Queen (yours, I mean) has been in San Francisco, arriving on the 24th of September to a royal salute of 21 guns and all the ships' flags dipped as the vessel Sacramento passed. Queen Emma was quickly conveyed to the Occidental Hotel, there being no other reception planned. All the city could muster was a street crowd of gawkers punctuated with an American baron or prince of commerce here and there. She dines privately with her attendants rather than show her royal self to the crowd in the public dining room where a good many folks with nothing regal about them but their jingling pockets wait to glimpse the woman they call "the barbarian queen"! She gives them no satisfaction, and it is just as well – the shock of her regal, well-dressed and graceful self would likely strike them dumb or dead.

I plan to gather the dispatches that I wrote for the Union *and string them together into a book while the excitement is high and anticipation soaring. "Mark Twain" incorporates some of that Hawaiian material into the lecture, advertising it as stories about "our fellow savages, the Sandwich Islanders." Never worry, dear one, that there is even a whisper about you, not an aside even, but of course beneath every breath is the fragrance of your name, the beauty of My Flower.*

If you have written, none of the missives have found me. Surely our letters have crossed in the mail. You must write to me. In my deepest heart, I ask your gods to keep you well and happy, my love.

Your Maka SLC

Emily understood Twain's leaving: his young ego had driven him. He had been afraid of losing "Mark Twain" in bliss and passion and ease. His identity was as yet too fragile for such surrender. Hawai'i could seduce one's spirit to abandon ego. That was Hawai'i's gift to willing travelers. But the journey had come too early in Twain's life for him to accept the gift. He had merely been running away from his troubles in the West. Once he had found Hawai'i, it was a matter of not being ready to see but only to look. He was offered answers to questions he did not ask. He'd had more knowledge than wisdom then. Emily hoped that she was not making the same error.

She understood that there was this difference between herself and Twain: she had come to Maui with her career secured, knowing the disappointment of having what you had been sure you wanted and had striven for only to find that it did not satisfy, in fact, it became a burden to maintain. Clemens had been on the other end of his success, when the lure of public acclaim and authorship had held him in thrall.

Emily turned again to the words Twain had written

for the *Sacramento Union* after he had left Maui: "six weeks since I touched a pen . . . never spent so pleasant a month before, or bade anyplace good-bye so regretfully . . . had a jolly time . . . would not have fooled away any of it writing letters." Emily could see that Mark Twain the writer was already warning his publisher and readers that he would not be writing again for five or six weeks, giving him time, she presumed, to find the words to cloak his sadness so no one would know. He also signaled that he would never write about those lost weeks. A "jolly time" he called it. He had already begun to translate the nights and days on Maui into an escapade, but underneath there was the word Emily heard most clearly: "regretfully."

December 14, San Francisco –

Dearest Napua,

I sail tomorrow for New York City on the ship America! I have been writing at white heat, 12 hours a day mostly, on the new book. It may seem that I am sailing in the wrong direction to return to you, dear flower, but there is work to be done and the public must be entertained and incited to buy my books. With that behind me, I shall once again steam westward and home to you. I am content to abide in winter for while, cold and sunless, longing for the better season and place, trusting in that invincible summer of the soul – and you. Until I can write again, aloha beloved.

SLC

"He meant to return, didn't he? It wasn't just one of those vacation romances." Emily's glance at Kamuela was obscured by gathering dusk but her voice insisted, "He loved her. If he had known about the child . . . "

"Then you wouldn't be doing research on Mark Twain. He would have been just another newspaper reporter in Honolulu or . . . we can't even imagine another life for him, can we? That is how it was meant to be. A garden cannot be a forest." They looked hard at the letters between them. "Tell me again why you can't stay."

"I have commitments back there in New York."

"Promises to keep . . . and miles to go . . . ." Kamuela sighed.

"It won't be like it was for them."

"How will it be for us, Emily?"

"I don't know yet."

"Let it be like this. Stay."

"I can't. I have to go back. Maybe you could come to New York?"

"Would you want me there?"

"Oh yes!"

"Together there or together here – together is what matters, yes? But what would I do there? Do they need a Hawaiian language teacher? Someone to dance hula?"

"I know. It wouldn't be fair. You are Hawaii. It doesn't translate very well to New York." They sat glumly holding hands in the half light. "And I can't stay here, not right now. Wait for me. I will come back. I promise." Generations of loss kept Kamuela from speaking. "Maybe you would rather not wait. Just tell me. Maybe it's time you married Loke. It's not too late, apparently. The keiki . . . think of children and being a father and the Homelands." He drew back, startled and a little angry. "JoJo told me," she explained.

"There are others in the ohana who will take care of that. I do not love Loke in that way. There was a time when I thought I should marry her, but when I was old enough, I knew I didn't love her in the way I needed to. Children – if they come – will spring from love, not duty, from the body of my beloved, from our joining, yours and mine. I have waited these years for you to come to me. I will wait to see if you come back."

"But your family – they don't accept me."

"Yet. It won't be easy for you, I know. But it has never been easy with anyone, has it?" She agreed but wondered at his knowing. "When I went away from the islands, to go to Oregon for college, Aunty Malia warned me about bringing back a haole wife and made much of me when I returned alone. She never knew that long before, when I was with the kahuna learning the old ways, a messenger came to me in dreams many times and told me that I was the one who would bring peace to the ohana. It used to seem as if that meant marrying Loke. Now I see it is to be with you, to live aloha, to help them learn to love you. And the hapa-haole keiki that may come. They need to learn to have aloha for more than just the land and their blood. The world is smaller each day. We can only survive by sharing our aloha, not cutting ourselves off. The whole world needs aloha." He breathed one long breath as if it had winded him to say so deep a thing. "But that is just the reason, and we don't reason where we love - we simply feel. I will wait for you to return."

The last weekend of July was fiercely hot. With schools reopening soon, everyone had gone to the beaches or the upcountry festivals for one last lick of summer vacation. Kamuela and Emily left the house early to miss the clotted roads and headed out toward Hana in his car, aiming for the Kaumahina Gulch, site of Clemens's first encampment with Napua. Emily traced the route with her finger on the map she had brought along, and she asked him for the third time how to spell the name of the place before he reached to take it from her gently and toss it into the backseat.

"It is not down on any map. True places never are."

Emily finally began to see the places she had missed on her first trip along this road, cascades and clefts, fruits and blossoms that flirted from within the green. When Kamuela pulled to a wide space on the roadside, she waited for him to lead her somewhere, *to* something. The gulch itself was hardly more than a dimple in the canopy that spread below the overlook, and no water was visible at all between the glint of a waterfall above them and the ocean below. Emily stepped closer to the ridge of rock that marked the farthest edge of the roadway, looking down the steep pitch of Haleakala's shoulder through a scrim of forest. Her foot slipped a bit on the wetness, and she tipped off-balance, grateful for Kamuela's hands pulling her back.

"I can't really see anything." She was disappointed and relieved. There was nothing to photograph or record, no scrap of hut that could become a tourist attraction.

"There is nothing of them left to see – not here." He noticed the line of sweat on her lip. "Are you ok?"

"Yes, just a little out of my body somehow." Her voice seemed to come from a long way, full of spider webs and distance. The heat buzzed around her. A red car passed them driving too fast, the top down exposing a pair of red-faced tourists. Before it was around the bend, another rental car sped by with a tour bus hugging its bumper. It swerved wide on the curve, grazing the air where they stood. "Would you like to go on to Hana?" He read the answer in her face. "Then how about a rodeo? There is the summer rodeo at Makawao." Soon more tourists would be surging along the narrow road trying to make the most of their time on Maui. Anything but the relentless stream of cars was her idea of pleasure, although a rodeo, even a Hawaiian cowboy, was not anything she could imagine. She tried to summon the images of the Maui ranch that Twain had visited but failed. "Or there's a beach luau – the *ohana* – if you wanted to."

"Were we invited?"

"Of course, but I didn't want to use the day making you unhappy."

"*Mahalo*, my love." She took in a steadying breath.

"I am ready for them now. But we have no food to take."

"You learn fast. Never go empty-handed. I know a place where we can pick up *kau kau* to take along. We will go."

Along the margin of the beach, under the shade of twisted *kiawe* trees, the assorted family vehicles were parked back-end to the ocean. Coolers and grills spilled onto the sand. The men of the family divided into parties of either grill masters or fishermen who worked their nets and lines out on the rocks. A bright blue tarp created deeper shade where babies could sleep on blankets piled on the sand, but mostly the precious *keiki* were dandled on a lap or cuddled in the crook of some relative's arm. On the tailgate of a truck, one of the young cousins picked at an ukelele, humming a song that Emily remembered from the night of the baby luau, a love song. Emily looked quickly to see if Aunty Malia or Loke was among the gathered clan, but suddenly she and Kamuela were ambushed by an old uncle with a wide hug. He pulled them toward the tables where she could not see either of the women. "It is good you come," the uncle bent his head to tell them softly. "The *ohana* will see and learn." With that, he released them into the quiet that had suddenly overtaken the laughter. The uncle laughed heartily before announcing their presence to the gathered Keana'aina *ohana*, cuing them to welcome Kamuela and his *wahine*. At the edge of the party, Loke rose and sauntered away from one of the young men and toward the ocean where the older children played.

Where the ocean made the sand wet and hard, Malia presided over youngsters who purred and giggled under her gentle hands and crooning story-voice. She looked up and nodded at Kamuela and Emily, her face wearing an expression Emily could not read, or perhaps no expression at all. Instead of joining the men, Kamuela led Emily to a clutch of cousins who made a place for them to perch and then resumed their "talking story." Easy chatter of pidgin embraced Emily, and she listened hard, laughing whenever they did, delighted that she was beginning to understand their soft patois. Kamuela moved his hand along her back, appreciating her, encouraging her. When the food was ready, the fishermen and *keiki* joined the handclasp circle while Kamuela blessed the food. They ate well, Emily tasting even the chunks of marinated raw fish they called "poke." An aunty drifted by and offered a quiet baby to Emily who dared not resist, although she had never particularly liked babies or found them interesting. Still, it was a pleasant weight on her arm, and it didn't cry as she expected but serenely laid its hand on her breast and stared at her. A cousin came along, and he and Kamuela greeted one another with the subtle jerk of the head. His green t-shirt screamed "It's a *kakou* thing" across the front. She asked Kamuela quietly what that meant. "Later," he muttered.

"Please."

"Ok – it's like saying 'It's a black thing,' except that it's a Hawaiian thing, a native thing, like *haoles* just wouldn't understand. Sorry, Em. He's just angry these days like a lot of the younger guys. Not enough jobs, Japanese in the legislature, a Filipino governor, *haoles* and Japanese running the university . . . ." Another cousin approached to ask Kamuela's advice about something the men were planning and they wandered away. Emily did not follow, holding the baby against her like a shield, until someone offered to take him.

The afternoon slipped into dusk with singing and stories. The women began to clear the food and coolers away, urging everyone to "make a plate." Abundant food meant that people took home another meal wrapped in tinfoil. Always there was the pride in having plenty. The fishermen bent by their ice chests comparing what remained of the day's catch without any real competition, pleased with each others' good fishing. When Emily tried to help clean up, the sisters and aunties were mildly surprised but gave her gentle direction. After watching awhile, Malia came to her side and took her by the wrist, leading her to an old *kiawe* tree that had been bent into a sort of bench by years of weather. Long thorns mingled with the tree's sweet bean fruit on the sand.

"How is your work coming along?" Malia's voice was crisp and low.

"Quite well. *Mahalo* for asking."

Malia did not acknowledge Emily's attempt with the language. "You will be going back to New York soon then." It was not a question.

"Yes, soon."

"And you and my nephew have agreed about the

journal." Again, it was not a question. "It is best that you return to New York. You see what you would have to give up to stay here with Kamuela. This is who he is. He must take his place in the *ohana*. He has responsibilities. Do you know where I was coming from that first time we met, on the plane? My daughter's oldest girl is a lawyer there in Chicago. We want her to come home. We need her here. There is much she can do for us, our people. Otherwise, fifty years from now, when Kamuela is old, a *kupuna* like me, there will be no real Hawaiians left on the land."

Emily refused to debate any of it. "I am going back to my work in New York." She hesitated telling the rest but couldn't resist, "and Kamuela will come to visit me at Thanksgiving." She was impressed by Malia's composure at this.

"So, do you think that New York will give him what he needs? Can you be *this* for him?" The sweep of her arm included the land, the ocean, and then the *ohana*.

"He will not stay in New York. He will come home. I know that. We will find our way."

"What is there here for you? No university, no family of your own, no land."

Behind them, Kamuela's voice was deep. "I will be her family, and my land will be hers. You underestimate her, aunty. She has a warrior spirit. She had to have that to become who she is, to do what she has done. She can teach us." He gripped Emily's hand and stood beside her, their equal heights making them a pair.

"Aloha isn't about bloodlines. You will see. The

world has grown too small for us to live as if it was."

Heat undulated above the tarmac, but inside the departure gate at the Kahului terminal, the air was too cold for them. Emily and Kamuela had already walked the length of the airport twice, barely talking but holding fast to each other. She had been tearful through too much of their last night and promised herself pointlessly that she would not weep today. They stood now leaning into each other's warmth at the barrier before the security checkpoint. On the other side of TSA, tired tourists and a few local inter-island passengers pressed toward the jetway. Soon the doors would yawn open and they would scurry aboard. Emily had no impulse to move. Airports had always been safe neutral spaces for her, perhaps because she had never felt that anyplace was home. Her goings and comings were full of the urgency to be somewhere else, always ahead of herself and never where her body was. Now she wanted only to remember and remain, knowing for certain where she was and why. She wanted nothing else but to walk away into that green dimness on the other side of the runway and be back where she might lay listening to the rain on the metal roof and watch Kamuela clean the fish he would have just caught. But July was gone, and there was so much to do in New York.

He had shown her what to do with the many *lei* that

he had given her, now only dried and crumpled flowers that she had kept without reflecting on why. They had gathered them from where she had strung them on the wall above the bed and taken them down to the beach last night, tossing them one at a time into the surge. "You must always give a *lei* back to the elements that created it. It is full of spirit - *mana* - and aloha. It angers me to see the tourists throw them into dumpsters - an insult. You can take them to the forest and hang them in the trees, or this . . ." he said, tossing one into the ocean.

"It doesn't surprise me that there are customs attached to leaving. So many people *do* leave, don't they? Hawaii is a destination, a port of call, and people fall in love with the romance of it, and then they go home or to some other port. What did you say the rule was? If the lei floats back to shore, it means I will return?"

Kamuela nodded and added, "Of course it almost always comes floating back - that's the way waves work."

"So it's a gimmick."

"People *do* come back. And some never leave." Kamuela pressed his hand on the small of her back. "But it is always easier to stay away than to go away."

"I have to go. But I will be one of the ones who comes back."

"Can you imagine how many times lovers have said that to our people?" She heard the exclusion in "our people" ricochet in the moment and was stung. "How many farewells and promises that were never kept? We are used to people coming and leaving, while we stay. And most of the time it doesn't matter. We give them our aloha, but we are careful who we love. We know that most will leave. There's always the going. Greeting and farewell. Aloha is so convenient that way, but love isn't."

She stood against the sun-washed greens in her khaki traveling clothes, functional and professional-looking again. Her skin was honey and peach now, but underneath was a paleness born of sorrow and regret. He had put a cluster of deep pink *plumeria* in her hair that morning before she was even out of bed. She wore the weight of fresh *lei* he had given her in the soft early light, draping them one at a time on her, reverently, tying the *maile* beneath her breasts before he kissed them. There was a braided *ti* leaf *lei* for safe travel given at the last moment and laid over the *pikake*. She took in the deep sweetness of the flowers.

"*Pikake* is my favorite, I think."

"It is the bride's flower."

"I remember." She also remembered the first *pikake* that he had picked for her from his aunt's garden, but Emily didn't want to think about the family guardian, choosing to sink into the scent and the memory of his marriage proposal, ignoring the impasse they were at over the diary. Emily had given it back to him. Not that he had asked for it. Weeks before he had surrendered to an imperative that Emily only sensed, more ancient and sacred than any reasoning she knew. He was content to watch the story unfold however it would, knowing that it had been destined a long time ago. She had finally told him that she had made a copy to take with her, explaining how she would use it, perhaps, and hoping maybe when she came back at Christmas the family would feel differently.

The steel doors to the jetway opened and the line surged toward it, but Kamuela and Emily did not move. When all the other departing passengers were gone, the woman in the airline aloha shirt muttered something to the TSA agent. One more kiss. Emily saw the wetness on Kamuela's face.

"You can't come back if you don't leave." He was resigned to her going.

She turned and tossed her bag and laptop toward the guard and did not look at Kamuela again before she hurried through the barriers and checkpoint and finally disappeared down the jetway. The steel door closed. Absence filled the cool glass room. And then there was a clatter as Emily pushed open the door and reappeared at the passageway beyond security. Behind Kamuela, the clutch of people who had come to see others off laughed delightedly at her return and what they thought was the triumph of romance. Emily waved a large manila envelope at the guard, now on high alert, and then pointed at Kamuela, and the guard finally took it from her and handed it across the jumble of agents and machines. A TSA agent looked inside at the xerox copy of the journal, figured it was harmless, and handed it to Kamuela.

"I'll come back! I promise!" Then she was gone again.

He knew without looking what was in the envelope. In a moment, he could just see her as she climbed over someone and into a window seat. He put his hand flat on the terminal's broad window where she might be able to see it. She pressed her own hand on the thick double pane of the plane's window as the jet backed away and taxied toward her past.

Emily Witt was more than early the day before Thanksgiving and waited inside the Buffalo airport out of the crisp air of late autumn. She wished she could wait for Kamuela at the gate where she could see and hold him almost as soon as he touched down, when the cold air and urban smells first hit him, but Homeland Security forbid that sort of passion, and she stood just behind the security gate. Outside the November day was gold and blue with the clear light that comes from living on the edge of lake water. Autumn had blustered in with too-warm days until suddenly an extravagance of colors like the evening skies in Maui erupted -- vermillion, aspen gold, maple reds. Emily was grateful to the gods of nature who ruled this corner of the planet for the drama of autumn color holding on. She wanted New York to be as beautiful as possible for Kamuela.

She let herself think about how he would look here and could not see him any way except as he had been on Maui. She touched her hair, fingering the length and wayward curves it fell into, and knew he would like the way it moved. The glint of summer sun and salt had lingered in the dark layers around her face. There was no trace of honey left on her skin, and she wondered if she would look to him as *haole* as the first day they met? She kept trying to see Kamuela coming toward her, how it would be, but the image eluded her. She leaned into the chilled concrete wall and imagined a different arrival.

Epilogue 1895

Clemens stood at the rail of the mail steamer *Warrimoo* looking hard through the dimness at a few lights on shore, unable to make out the shape of Diamond Head, though he knew it was there. They would lay off port tonight, having steamed across the Pacific these last seven days but arrived too late for landing at Honolulu today. From out at sea, there seemed to be little difference in the town as he remembered it, though he knew that the changes of almost three decades had been great. He had read every dispatch he could find in the newspapers and squeezed anyone who might have bits of news, but most was about the triumph of cane, the "Sugar is King" sort of story, and too often a royal funeral. The last queen, Lili'uokalani, had been deposed two years before in a bloodless coup led by American businessmen. He wondered what *haole* decadence had replaced the honest harmony of Hawaii under its monarchs, how his beloved islands might be changed. Finally he resolved that it did not matter. He would rather be there than any place on earth. The moon hung above him in a narrow crescent flinging shards of silver onto the sea. They barely relieved the darkness.

He went below and shrugged into his berth, but sleep eluded him. Livy slumbered deeply a few steps away in her adjoining cabin, tired with her wifely work of loving him through his mercurial disposition these days and absorbing as much of the social responsibilities as she could to lighten his moods. This round-the-world tour and the hope of earning enough money to quiet his creditors weighed on him. There had been so many losses. Maintaining the house in Hartford was costing more than he had calculated. The lavish hospitality to a steady flow of visitors, the extravagant entertainments and soirées, and then the failure of the Paige typesetting machine had bled away all his reserves and resources. It was beginning to seem that bankruptcy was the only way out except leaving America behind for a cheaper, bohemian style of living in Europe. All the world seemed contemptible and greedy these days except for one sea-girt haven he remembered. The dismal accommodations, a sloppy crew and unappetizing food seemed trifles as he drew closer to Hawai'i. This voyage might bring solvency and comfort for the family, but to himself he admitted that the greater lure was the opportunity to finally return to Hawaii. He was no mere traveler this time, no tourist with letters of introduction, not a reporter, but a pilgrim.

With the disappointments and deaths of years, he

saw now that he had been mistaken about his island Eve. It would have been better to stay in the Garden with her than toil all this time outside of it and without her. It would have been kinder, too, for him not to wrench Livy's life with care and desperation as well. Since leaving Vancouver and land, he had been suspended, almost out of reach of all the struggle and bother, the sorrows that plagued him back there, the many nets that had caught and held him all these years, and the specter of financial ruin. Five hundred tickets had already been sold for his Honolulu lecture, and he would leave that money with Livy. Now his escape was nearly complete.

Well before dawn, a dream startled him awake, a nightmare of appearing before his audience in nothing more than his shirt, otherwise naked fore and aft. Rising with the hint of light, he laid aside his dark blue traveling suit, dressed himself carefully in his white tropical trousers and jacket and smoothed his hair, now long past the russet blaze of twenty-nine years before. Going out, he bypassed breakfast, hungry only for the feel of this land beneath his feet once more. This land. His heart turned over in his breast. The memory of rapture swept over him, and his hands trembled on the buttons of his white coat. He strained to see through the twilight. Hawaii lay before him again, but he came to her this time without the callow self-indulgence of early manhood. At sixty, he was no longer the young journalist for hire. He came this time as lover and exile, coming home. He yearned across the double distance to her shores, this present and that long-ago day that this landing had become his dream. A seaman scurried past, the one he privately called "Pockets" for one of his habits. Clemens accosted him in mid-step down a stairway. "When shall we land, lad? What time does the first tender go?"

"We're not going to be able to land, Mr. Twain. There's cholera ashore."

The man in white whirled on the youth who delivered the sentence.

"Who says so?"

"The captain, sir. Pilot boat came out just before sunrise and says no one's allowed ashore. Cholera, sir. We can't even take on provisions or mail. Damnedest thing. Eighty-eight cases. Five dead just yesterday. Mostly native, though." The sailor stood staring at Honolulu with his hands thrust contemplatively into his pockets.

"But I must go ashore."

"Sorry, sir, the captain says . . ."

"Who is the launch waiting for then?"

"Residents, Mr. Twain. But the captain says no one can land, just the folks who only booked this far – final destination passengers."

Final destination was precisely what he wanted.

"You're James, aren't you?"

"Yes sir, at your service, Mr. Twain."

"And the service I want, James, is to get ashore—somehow. You can manage that, right? There must be a way. I'll line those pockets you're so fond of if you'll get me ashore."

"I can't, Mr. Twain. Cholera! My god, you wouldn't

chance it!"

"You may be worried about dying and going to heaven, but I'll stay here instead. Just put me ashore. Alone."

"But the ship will be leaving shortly - we've got to get on to Fiji and take on provisions, then make the run for Australia." The insistence in his voice attracted the attention of two other gentlemen who had risen early to smoke their cigars before their wives joined them for breakfast. A brief explanation from the seaman and they were off to tell the news.

Clemens gripped the solid wood of the rail and measured the distance to shore with his heart. He considered his choices. He remembered another voyage when he had attempted the leap from the boat back to the embrace of paradise, but now he was too old. The morning rose behind him, lighting his figure in white relief against the emerald hills. The afternoon would bring clouds to the tops of the mountains, but in this early light of day, all of Oahu was green, here and there just a glimpse of a Honolulu street below the sweeping treetops and steeples rising above it all. He had spent twenty-nine years speaking in curves, keeping the secret alive and hidden in his heart while he went along, getting the fame he couldn't live without, never able to tell it straight out, the way it had been on Maui, making light of it sometimes, and in unguarded moments, or when he felt that it was safe, he said the words they heard about Hawaii's beauty and soul. But no one knew, ever, that there was once a woman who was Hawaii to him, and she had taught him how to love beyond race and time, here and hereafter. Now he was to be exiled again, not by ambition this time, but kept at bay like a leper bound and shipped and helpless. In the clear water below, two sharks lazed in the shadow of the hull.

Livy had caught the news below decks. Her familiar pallor was exaggerated by the early light as she came out of the gaping passageway onto the deck. The years of marriage may have dimmed her dark eyes and pewtered her hair, but the luminous beauty of her countenance endured. Mark Twain had married the perfect wife – frail, pale and pious - and heiress to a half a million in coal profits. Livy had claimed a place in his heart and his work, and now she had not only tamed him but kept him more or less (and generally more) on a path of social and moral reform. His frequent lapses and pledges to do better had created a career for Livy. Without their ever discussing it, she had always known that he had experienced Hawai'i the way some men feel religion. Now to be merely sailing past the islands must be a crucifixion for him. And there was the five hundred or so dollars he lost by not being able to lecture in Honolulu. Livy sagged under the weight of her duty, but she went to him at the rail. His shoulders heaved, and she feared some sickness.

But it was only longing. Napua would always be there in the islands, heart-free and young, but he must finally submit to years and old necessities. The cigar fell from his fingers. He would live as if he had never known that other life, that Paradise. He would do his duty. Perhaps Livy was right and Heaven was just like

Hartford but without the debts, some domestic realm where kin and kith would be reunited in bridled bliss. Heartsick and weary with his living, he looked beyond the harbor to the green-backed hills. He turned to Livy, resigned to her piety and comfort, knowing he would never make the shore.

CPSIA information can be obtained at www.ICGtesting.com
Printed in the USA
BVOW010650011211

277228BV00001B/4/P